A BROKEN EVERYTHING

EDDIE WRIGHT

LUV.

Prologue

I want to be good now. I want to be right now. I want to be happy now. Happiness can play if you let it out into the yard. Mine's grounded. Mine said, "fuck" and I washed its mouth out with soap and it's in its room. I want to let the happiness out but the happiness needs to learn to stop being such a goddamn smart-ass.

There's peace in me. There's real in me. There's life in me. I think of these things and that means these things are there. If they weren't there, then I wouldn't think of them. I wouldn't even know what they are. Misery is worthless and that's the new way to think. That's the right way to think. That's the way I want to live. That's the way I'm going to live.

Starting now.

Happy.

Peace.

Great.

Okay. That's done. I'm happy. I'm a different person now. I'm good now. I'm right now.

And it feels great.

It feels really great. I'm smiling and good and people want to love me. People want me to love them. I want to love and be loved and love love. Loving lovebugs are crawling all over my face and climbing into my nose and walking on my eyeball like a starving kid in Africa. I want to feed that kid. I want that kid to be fat and healthy and then I want to eat him. Because I'm starving. I'm starving for good. Doing good would be good and I want to eat the good. I want to eat the right. I want to eat the peace. I want to eat the optimism and puke the pessimism. I want to shit negativity. I want to cleanse. I want to be clean. I want to drink some of that dumb juice and cleanse myself and purge myself and be a wispy, frothy, hollow dream, floating on a cloud of smiles.

Oh, I'm good and it feels good.

I feel right.

I feel peace.

I feel God coursing through veins.

God is in my balls.

God is in my ass.

God is down my throat.

God is hugging me and it's beautiful and I'm kissing Him with tongue. I'm sucking on His beard. He's dipped His beard in glory and I'm sucking it from the hair. The hair is stuck in my teeth but I love it. I'm yanking each one out and swallowing it down and loving my belly and loving the love and loving digestion and digesting love.

Oh, God's love is good.

God's love is great.

God's love is love with a capital LOVE.

Hearts beating. Hearts pounding. Hearts shattering and

growing into new hearts. And those hearts are shattering and growing into new hearts and shattering and growing and shattering and growing until the strongest most excellent heart has grown and enveloped my face and my face is a giant beating heart squirting juices of love all over everyone I see. They'll hate it at first but then they'll love it. They'll run through the streets puking juice of love into the gutters. And the gutters will run with love and wash into the sea and love waves will crash into the shore and the sand and the earth and the cycle of life will be infected with love. And love will rain upon us. And it will be because of me. And everyone will love me and everyone will thank me and everyone will be my friend. And I will be the change. I will be the angel. I will be the prophet. I will be the justice. I will be the love.

I am the love.

I am the peace.

I am the right.

I am the good.

My name is Daniel Groff and this is not my story.

Part One

CHAPTER ONE

The Confabulations of Daniel Groff

Sometimes I listen to music and pretend that the person singing is me and I'm allowing someone to hear my new demo tape that I made using a program on my computer. I still call it a demo "tape" despite it being a demo "ones and zeroes" because that makes me seem like an authentic, old school artist who knows something about recording music prior to the twenty-first century with all its digital whateverness. I also tell myself/them that I played all the instruments except the drums. I do this because I'm happy to admit that I don't know how to play the drums and I wouldn't want to misrepresent myself. Drums seem hard to play. I tell them/me that the drums are electronic beats which I programmed. I don't know how to program electronic drum beats either. I don't know how to play any instruments at all. I don't know how to write songs. I don't want to know how to write songs but I wish I knew how to write songs. And I wish I could record them using a program on my computer and I could let people hear them. I could record videos singing heartfelt renditions of my songs and upload them to the internet and people that I don't know or care about would virtually pat me on the back and I would feel good and feel afraid of releasing the next song because people liked the first song and I'd feel arrogant and cocky and full of shit because ten people told me that I'm a good songwriter and ten people loved me and needed me and wanted me and cared about me. And then I'd put up the new song and no one would respond. And no one would care. And those ten people would no longer like me. And I wouldn't like me.

I already don't like me.

I can't make art.

That's why this is not art.

This is me being me as not being me so I can be a better me.

Does that make sense?

Fuck it.

This is bullshit.

This is stupid.

Okay?

Okay.

We're here now.

And my mother knocks on my door.

"Daniel?" she calls.
"What is it?" I say.
"Can you open this please?"
My dresser is barricading the door. I'm writing and I'm drinking and it's my room and it's my time and I don't want any visitors.
"What do you want?" I ask.
"It's important, Daniel. I need to tell you something."
I pause for a several seconds and think. I feel anxious. I feel strange. I feel annoyed.

"Now!" she yells.

A few years ago, I published my first book, *The Psycho Killer Down the Street*. It's a series of short stories about a kid who fights a psycho killer down his street and eventually goes to Hell and fights Satan. I actually wrote the stories when I was in the third grade. I found them in a box in the attic of the house I live in with my mother. I found them and read them and liked them. They were pretty good (especially for a third grader) and I remember my teacher Mr. Biggsman liked them back in 1989. He said I had promise. He said it I had "it." He said I was cool.

Mr. Biggsman was a good person. He's probably dead now.

So I typed them into a computer program, printed them, stapled them, and sent them away in manilla envelopes to have them professionally published. But when I sent the book to publishers and agents and people in suits with offices, I got nicely typed letters like this:

Dear Mr. Groff,

We would love to publish your book, *The Psycho Killer Down the Street*, but unfortunately we can't, because simply speaking, it is not very good. We have a strict policy of not publishing poopy books, and your book is a super-poopy, poopy book. Honestly, after reading it, we hate you, Mr. Groff. We hate you with the fury a hundred, million fires and we hope you die. Now go ahead and do that please, Mr. Groff. Okay? Die, Mr. Groff. Die! Die! Die!

Here is a list of other things we hate, besides your book, in case you were wondering (in no particular order, of course):

1. Whales
2. Dancing
3. Christmas
4. Magic
5. Keanu Reeves movies

Now go fucking die.

Best of luck in any and all future endeavors. Dickhead.

Sincerely,
Marcus Newman
Newman Books

I used this website that lets people upload writing and sell books through the internet to losers with dumb taste. It's called self-publishing. Now I'm a published author. According to my internet stats, I sold a book to a stranger. His username was BELUGA_WHALE_69. I've thought about looking him up.

And I've been working on a second book (well, I guess it's technically a first book since I wrote that other one when I was nine, and I didn't even know it was a book when I was writing it, but whatever). Something keeps holding me back, though. I want my second book to be a detective story and I want it to feature a confident detective and I want him to investigate a murder or a disappearance or something like that. I want the main character to be relaxed and calm and cool and collected and strong and real and clever and quippy. I want this to happen because there's something in me that needs that. But something is stuck in me and it's blocking that thing I need. And I can't get that something unstuck. I think that something that's stuck is something bad. Fucking bad things are stuck in me and they won't get out of me. The bad things are in me and I want them out of me. Fuck fucking bad things. Fuck them gently into the dark. I think this may be writer's block but I don't know what writer's block feels like. Does it feel like constipation in your face? Does it feel like bad things? If it does, I think I've got it. Bad things create things that are the opposite of fictional, fantasy detective men who are relaxed and calm and cool and collected and strong and real and clever and quippy. Bad things are stupid and create stupid, insecure, neurotic assholes with stupid, insecure, neurotic asshole faces.

Faces like mine.

The Psycho Killer Down the Street will be featured in its entirety within the pages of the book you are currently reading. I'll do this for two reasons: the first is to make it easier for you to understand who *The Psycho Killer Down the Street* is, the second is to pad out this book so it's longer and I feel like I accomplished more. If this book is big and thick then I'll feel successful and legitimate and real. Like an author. Like a real author. I'm lazy and I don't like to think of new things to write so I'm going to repeat myself.

So here I go, repeating myself.

So here I go, repeating myself.

"Daniel Groff, OPEN THIS FUCKING DOOR!" mom yells.

I sigh, screw the cap on my bottle of Lonely Sparrow Whiskey, and jam it in a drawer. I leave my desk, push the dresser to the side, unlock the dead bolt, and open the door.

"WHAT!" I shout.

My mother's eyes are full of tears as she tells me that my father is dead. She wraps her arms around me. My hands remain at my sides.
"Your father hated sitcoms," she says.
I tug at my pants until I can feel the moisture developing on my palms.
"Your father hated pork chops."
My father was a man who used to live with me and my mother. His name was Daniel Groff too. I'm a junior. He used to be a cop but he retired. Not sure why. Never bothered to ask. But it was before I was born. He popped a lot of pills and spent a lot of time locked in his room working on his "projects." God knows what those "projects" were. But when we did see him he would yell and scream and throw all the pots and pans and plates and bowls on the floor. He would push hot spaghetti in mom's face if she asked too many questions during dinner. He would break her nose if she disagreed about a TV show. And he would throw all of her clothes onto the front lawn if she took too long at the grocery store.

He was a bully, he was a brute, and he destroyed mom in ways that I'll never know. He wasn't good. And it's as simple as that.

Then he left us.

And I hadn't seen him or thought about him for years. Certain things would remind me of him though. Certain smells, certain sounds, certain stories. Those reminded me of the good things. While few and far between, there were some. There was playing in the backyard, hiking in the woods, baseball games on the couch. Things like that. Those things were good. But the good inevitably reminded me of the bad: the insanity, the pills, the violence, the ugly.

He liked the ugly.

Mom tells me to put on my suit. I don't do a good job of tying the tie. I try several times but it keeps ending up too short. I sigh and button my jacket to cover it.

We get in the car and drive to the funeral. There are a lot of people there; mostly family, but a few strangers too. It's an uncomfortable situation because people keep coming up to me and hugging me and shaking my hand and kissing me and telling me how sorry they are.

They're sorry. They're sorry. They're sorry. They're sorry.

For what?

I don't know. But one man in the back of the room keeps staring at me. Like he knows me and has got something to say to me. He looks about fifty-something. He's balding, chubby, has a mustache, and looks like a bum. He's wearing sunglasses and I notice that he has food on his face. It looks like tuna. Whenever anyone eats tuna there's always a little left over on the face. Tuna's a food that likes to hang around. It likes to stick to the outside. It doesn't want to be swallowed-up. If I was a food, I would be tuna.

This man is wearing a suit. But underneath the suit and pale-blue dress shirt, I notice he's wearing a Hawaiian shirt. Which means he's wearing two button-up shirts on top of each other.

That's a strange thing to do. It also doesn't sound comfortable. I guess he likes to know that his laidback self is always around, even when it's covered up by fancy attire. I figure that this man is not in big business. He's not a CEO or stock market person. He probably makes hamburgers. Maybe he paints dollhouses. Maybe he's a tuna fisherman. Maybe he has no job. Like me.

He keeps staring and I stare back. Perhaps he knew me when I was a kid. Perhaps he's about to approach me and hand me a dollar and tell me he's my uncle who recently got out of jail and remembers me from when I was the size of a peanut and missed me and loves me even though he doesn't know me. Extended family love is weird because extended family love is fake. You love an uncle because you have to, because you feel obligated, not because you do. If you had a bomb shelter with a small amount of space and enough food rations to feed three or four people I guarantee that you would leave your aunts and uncles outside to fend off the atomic fallout, or zombies, or tornadoes, or whatever. Extended family members don't get spots in bomb shelters. It's a fact.

As I wait in line to look at the body I realize that I'm behind the man. He doesn't acknowledge me. I figure this would be a good time for him to talk to me and tell me all about how when I was little he took me hunting and I killed an elephant and how we ate tusk until we puked. Or I thought maybe he'd tell me about the time when I was two and he gave me beer and I got drunk and drove a car into a pool. But no, I'm wrong. There's nothing from Uncle Double-Shirt. No stories. No nothing.

He makes his way to the body, kneels before the casket, bows his head, and mutters a Hail Mary. He slowly raises his head, leans forward, and kisses my father on the mouth. I hear him whisper something but can't make out the words. He makes the sign of the cross, rises by bracing himself on the edge of the box, and stiffly walks away. I approach my dead dad, take a knee, and stare. His hands are laid on top of one another and his suit is clean and perfectly pressed. As I look closer at his waxy face, I notice something in the corner of his mouth: tuna. The man has left a piece of tuna on my father's face. I quickly look for him and lock my eyes with his shades as he stands calmly in the corner. After a second or two of solid staring he nods. I return the nod and he turns and walks out of the funeral home. I take one more look at my father, get to my feet, and follow the man outside.

CHAPTER TWO

The Psycho Killer Down the Street

Daniel Groff Jr.
Grade 3
October 11, 1989

One day, I was hanging around. I was listening to a big fight from the house down the street. This guy lives there. Nobody really sees him but I've seen him a few times. His face has a big scar on it. My friends have never seen him. They think he's just a cranky old man, but I know he's some kind of nut. My friends always say I'm wasting my time watching this guy's house but I've dealt with people like this before.

My friends dared me to go up to the house so I did because I always take a dare. As soon as I walked up to the guy's porch my friends ran away laughing. The guy's lawn was all dry and there were dead bushes everywhere. I knocked on the door and a hand grabbed me by my throat and pulled me inside.

As soon as I was inside the guy threw me against the wall then ran upstairs and dove out a closed window. I ran out the door and chased him down the street. He took out a gun and fired two shots at me. Luckily, he missed. He ran to Main Street and he shot someone off a motorcycle and stole it. I saw another one on the side of the street so I borrowed it. I got on and started chasing him. He shot my tire and I crashed through someone's house. I got up and took a steak knife out of their kitchen and threw it as hard as I could at his tire and it popped his tire and he slid down a hill into a manhole. I ran and jumped into the manhole. He slapped me in the face and took out a knife that had the word PSYCHO scratched onto it. He hit my head against the sewer wall. Suddenly water started pouring onto us. I was really bleeding. He sliced my face and arm. I kicked him in the face. Then he threw me against the wall. I had to get him! I jumped on the ground and pulled the gun out of his holster and shot him in the back. He's dead. Here comes the cops.

The End?

CHAPTER THREE

Kiddo

Uncle Double-Shirt stands on the sidewalk, staring into traffic. He looks straight ahead and allows the cars to pass through his line of sight. As I step into the bright sun, I watch him. He gradually inches his way to the curb until the toes of his tweed loafers dangle over the street.

From the inside pocket of my suit jacket, I pull my bottle of Lonely Sparrow Whiskey, unscrew the cap, swig, and yell to the man, "I like your Hawaiian shirt!"

There's no response.

I try again, "I'd like to go to Hawaii someday."

Nothing.

I stuff the bottle into my pocket and approach. "How do you know my father?" I say.

He continues to stare as I make my way to him.

"How do you know my father?" I repeat.

"I don't," he whispers.

"Then why are you at his funeral?"

"Why are you?"

"My mother brought me."

"Why?"

"Because my father is dead."

"Why?"

"Why what?"

"Why did he die?"

"Because people do that."

"But why did he have to die?"

"I don't know."

He turns to face me and removes his shades. His eyes are large and seem unable to focus. They're locked in a gaze slightly over my head. They're watery and it looks as if the man has severe allergies. Or is severely stoned.

"Are you okay?" I ask.

He slowly rotates his eyeballs until his hazy pupils meet mine. "Do you want to?" he says.

"Do I want to what?"

"Do you want to know why Daniel Groff had to die?"

"Sure."

He grabs my lapels like he's about to slug me and pulls me close. He presses his nose against my cheek and he whispers quickly, "Because It needs us. It needs our parts. It needs them for itself. But we need them more. We need them because they're our parts. It wants to make them Its parts because sometimes our parts make sense with Its parts. When it is time, you know it's time. It's not always what It says It is. It's not what you always think."

"I'm not sure I—"

"Shut up now," he says, placing his hands against the sides of my face, staring into my eyes. "There's a river beneath our feet. Do you hear it? Do you feel it?" His eyes whip from my left eye to my right quickly and erratically. Like he's scanning me.

"No," I say.

"Lane Laszlo," he says.

"Lane Laszlo?"

The man smiles and giggles. "You'll know, kiddo. Yup, yup, yup, you'll know." And the man licks from my chin to my nose. His breath reeks of tuna and it makes me sick when his tongue slides over my lips.

"Oh god!" I shout and pull away, wiping my hand across my mouth.

The man steps back and extends his arms outward. "The truth is with you, kiddo! Yup, yup, yup, the truth is with you!"

And the man happily steps into traffic.

I watch his body roll up the hood of a car and crash into the windshield. His limbs flop like a sock monkey. His sunglasses sail through the air, tumbling, twirling, and twisting toward me. They land near my feet and I lift them by the black plastic arm. I stare at them and think of my father's body in the casket. He didn't look real. He didn't look dead. Why do people find death more appealing when the dead person looks alive? They should lay a rotting corpse in the room. We should be able to smell it. We should be able to taste it. Sagging skin and drooping eyes and dead-guy stink would make more impact. People would feel the death, not see it. Death should float in the room like a cloud of mosquitoes. You should be able to touch the death. It should be able to bite you. It should suck your blood.

And I look at the man's body and watch his limp frame slide from the hood to the street. He hits the pavement with a thud that registers in the lowest part of my bowels. It's a gross sound. It's a sound that makes you go, "Oooooo."

Blood pours from his mouth in a slimy strand of redness and I look to the sunglasses again.

"Lane Laszlo," I say.

And I slide the glasses onto my face.
"Lane Laszlo. I like the sound of that."

CHAPTER FOUR

The Birdhouse

They tell me, "I'm very sorry for your loss." I fucking hate sympathy cards. I don't care if someone cares. I don't care if someone is sorry. It wasn't their fault. They didn't kill my father. I don't know what killed my father but it certainly wasn't Aunt Misty and her one-eyed dog, Cakeface. It wasn't Ms. Weincracker my ninth grade biology teacher. It wasn't Gordy and Swampass, my drooling, disgusting "friends" from Cub Scouts.

Along with the cards, there's an official-looking, non-sympathy envelope. I tear it open and read. It's a letter typed on thick paper that tells me my father left me his house. My body warms to the point of discomfort as I read the words. I don't even know where his house is. I've never been there. I've never seen it. How do I know if I want it? What if it sucks? What if it's stupid? What if it smells? What if it's haunted? What if the neighbors are idiots? What if there's a fire? What if I get robbed? What about earthquakes? What about tsunamis and hurricanes and floods and tidal waves? What if it's in a rough neighborhood? I could never survive that. I could never make it.

And I drop the letter, guzzle the Lonely Sparrow, peel off my clothes, and climb in the shower. I run the water and clutch my knees and stare into the drain. I breathe the steam and close my eyes and think.

Peace and quiet.

Privacy.

Solitude.

Like this.

I'll have nothing but time to think and read and write. No more of Mom's reality shows. Peace and quiet. Peace and quiet is what a writer needs. I can finally start smoking cigarettes. I can finally dangle a burning butt from my lip while I type furiously like a guy from the '40s. I can flick the finished ones on the floor and never pick them up. I can bounce a ball against the wall like Jack Nicholson in *The Shining*. I can have a party. I can set traps like that kid in *Home Alone*. I can get drunk and fall down the stairs. I can masturbate in the living room. I can finally be the writer I always wanted to be. I can finally work and do real work and make real things and change it all.

And the water turns cold and I decide to get out and I've made up my mind.

I pack my room and pack my clothes and Mom and I get in the car.
"You know how to get there?" I ask her.
"Yes, I know about it from before," she says.
"When?"
"Before."
"Before when?"
"Before he died. Here we go."
And she puts the car into drive and we drive. I stare out the window and prepare to settle into a state of delirium when Mom says, "We're here."
I look at her confusedly, then check the window and see the house. It's big and old and the grass is brittle and it looks like it might've been nice once, but is now dying. There's a man in a suit on the front steps. I get out of the car and look back and see our apartment building roughly five hundred feet away. Mom gets out of the car and stands by her door.
"Are you sure this is right, Mom?"

"What do you mean? 7 Milberg Place. This is it. I told you I've seen it before."

"But..." I look from my father's house to our building and back to the house.

"Come on, get your stuff," she says.

I open the trunk and remove the box that contains my possessions and walk to the front door.

The guy in the suit extends his hand for a shake.

"Mr. Groff, I'm Trig Fallstaff, I'm a lawyer."

"Weird name."

"Thank you, Mr. Groff. Weird names are interesting."

"I guess."

"Yes, you do."

I shrug.

"Cool box," he says.

The giant cardboard box is full of special somethings: comic books, horror movie action figures, some underwear, a few t-shirts, a computer, and several hundred sheets of paper covered in notes, ideas, short stories, and unintelligible nonsense. I'm still wearing my suit from the funeral. It's comfy and I've been sleeping in it.

The lawyer continues to hold out his hand and I try to rest the weight of the box in my left hand and on my knee to free my right hand to shake. I nearly fumble the box, but catch it before it tumbles.

"I can't shake hands with you right now, lawyer."

He doesn't drop the hand. "Why don't you put the box on the ground so we can shake hands?" he says.

"Why?"

"It's important to shake hands, Mr. Groff. I'm a lawyer. It's important to me."

"I know, but..."

"Have you been drinking, Mr. Groff?"

"What's it to you?"

The lawyer smiles and stares. And pisses me off.

"Put the box down," he says.

I sigh and place the box on the patio and stand to face him.

"See, that wasn't hard."

"Whatever," I say. We shake hands.

"I'm sorry for your loss," he says.

"I suppose you are."

"You're welcome," he says with an awkward smile and continues to shake my hand, jiggling my body like I'm sitting in a vibrating chair in one of those stores in the mall.

"Were you close with your father?" the lawyer asks after finally releasing his grasp.

"No."

"When's the last time you saw him?"

"When's the last time you saw yours?"

"Earlier today," he smiles. "We went horseback riding."

"Oh, isn't that nice?"

"It was wonderful. Such powerful animals."

"So are lawyers."

"Ha!" Fallstaff shouts and stares uncomfortably.

I stare back.

"So your pop left you this house, huh?" he says, presenting the junky, falling down heap behind us like a *Price is Right* spokesmodel.

"Seems like it."

"It's nice," he says with an insincere nod, "fixer-upper."

"Handyman's dream."

"Are you handy… man?" he says.

"Not at all."

"Oh, good! Then you'll be right at home."

I eye the papers in the lawyer's hand. "You got something for me to sign?"

"Why yes, I do," he says and hands me a fancy pen that feels like it weighs ten pounds.

He flips through the pages and points to the X's and I sign. I notice that my signature is rarely the same again and again. It's almost as if different people have signed my name twelve different times. I don't really have what would be called a signature signature. Sometimes it's neat and sharp. Sometimes it's grand and graceful like it belongs on The Declaration of Independence. Sometimes it's a reckless squiggle like a doctor. Sometimes it's slow and sloppy like a little boy who recently learned cursive in school. Sometimes I write a D.

The lawyer takes the pen and the papers, shakes my hand again, slaps me on the arm, sprints to his car, and drives away. I watch until he's out of sight and I pick up the box and walk through the front door of my new house.

There's a lot of brown and it smells like cigarettes and wetness. There are holes in the walls, faded outlines where picture frames once hung, and white furniture that's covered in stains and burns. The house feels like it's from another time.

Mom follows me. She's carrying a box of old kitchen things that she wants me to have. She cautiously looks around like a booby trap could spring on her at any second. Her face is damp with nervous sweat. She looks sad and scared and I wonder why she didn't drop me off and leave. She brings the box into the kitchen and slowly puts the pots and pans and plates and forks and spoons and knives into cabinets and drawers. I watch her until she squats and disappears behind an open cabinet door and I notice an old oak desk. It's nice and beat-up and chipped and has coffee ring stains on it. It's dusty and I like it a lot. I place my finger on it and draw a D. There are several drawers and I look through them. All of them are empty except one. There's a pack of Kools cigarettes and a Zippo lighter adorned with a silver police badge (number 1216). I flip the lid on the lighter, spin the wheel, and ignite the flame. I stare at it for a beat, close the lid, and drop the lighter into the inside pocket of my suit jacket. I take the pack of smokes, notice there are still a few left, sniff the tobacco, and place them in my pants pocket.

"For later," I say and set up the computer.

After the monitor is set and the keyboard and mouse are placed nicely on the desk, I plug the monitor and computer into a surge protector and stick the cord into the nearest outlet and press the power button on the PC tower.

Nothing happens.

I remove the cord and jam it into the outlet underneath the

first.

Nothing.

I take an extension cord from the cardboard box and plug the surge protector cord into one end, run it across the room, and stick the other end into an outlet.

Still nothing.

There seems to be no electricity in the room.

I sit cross-legged on the floor and think. Is it my responsibility to have the power turned on in the house? I wonder if since it's my house, I'm also expected to take care of such contrivances as mowing the lawn, and fixing the plumbing, and paying for heat, and fixing broken things, and getting the mail, and getting the paper, and making lunch, and making dinner, and paying bills, and answering the phone, and bathing regularly, and washing my clothes, and drying my clothes, and ironing my clothes, and talking to neighbors, and getting married, and having babies, and having a family, and getting a Christmas tree, and putting up Christmas lights, and having Thanksgiving dinner, and handing out candy to trick-or-treaters, and watching kids grow up, and retiring, and playing golf, and playing cards, and wearing cologne, and wearing a watch, and loving my wife, and kissing her mouth, and holding her hand, and touching her boobs, and being a homeowner, and dying. I wonder if these things are now expected of me.

Then I realize that I should check for a fuse box.

I get up and wander down the hall. I open the first door I find. It's a closet. There are two leather jackets, which smell bad and turn my stomach. There's also a broom, a few boxes, and a pair of boots. I close the door and move on.

The next door is a bathroom. It smells damp and old person-y. The faucet drips gently and rhythmically. The toilet has a brown ring around the top of the water. The shower walls are growing mildew. The mirror is spotty and I notice a toothbrush in a cup on the sink. I lean closer and see that the bristles are split and frayed. The toothbrush is too old to be used and it needs to be replaced. I grab it from the cup and toss it in the garbage can next to the toilet. I glance at my reflection and leave the room.

There's another door at the end of the hall. I try to open it, but something is blocking it. This is probably the crazy person recluse room that's full of thousands of newspapers and dead animals. I don't feel like dealing with that now. I decide to move on.

The next door reveals a dark, dingy staircase that looks like it leads down to a basement. It's dusty and my nose feels the way it would feel if I was about to sneeze. But no sneeze comes. The dust remains stuck within my nose hair. The semi-sneeze radiates from my nose into my cheeks and upwards to my eyeballs. They are watering and itching. I quickly rub my palms on my face in a rapid, repetitive up-and-down motion like I'm trying to warm a hypothermic limb. I take a breath and forge ahead.

I step down onto the wood slowly and carefully. Each step creaks like a squawking parrot. Each step begs me for a cracker. Each step tells me to fuck myself in an adorable little cartoon voice. Each step leads me to somewhere and to something that makes my heart pump a little faster. It's dark, it's uncertain, it's confusing.

As my foot hits the cement floor, I take the lighter from my pocket and flip the flame. A halo surrounds me and illuminates the nastiness. It's a basement that looks like a basement. An ugly basement. There are things, there's moisture, there's darkness, there's creepiness, there's crap.

I hold the flame like a torch in a jungle. I scan the walls but find nothing but exposed beams and fiberglass. There's dampness in the air and I feel it on my skin and in my hair. I walk the perimeter of the room, ducking ducts and stepping over moldy cardboard boxes that droop from the wetness of the underneath world. I think of rats and mice and roaches and silverfish. I think of snakes, bats, goblins, and darkness. I think of scary things and creatures and monsters and slime. I start to scare myself. I start to shake. I start to breathe. I think of leaving and turn to go when I find a doorway tucked in the back corner of the basement that leads to another, smaller room.

The lighter lights the way as I step through the door. I notice the walls are decorated with pieces of paper and scraps and junk. I hold out the flame and approach a sign written in magic marker that hangs in the center of the wall. It says:

ELECTRICITY IS THE PROBLEM AND THE SOLUTION!!!

I slide my fingers under the sign and pull it from the wall. I read it again and I look up and see that beneath it is the fuse box. I drop the sign, open the small door, and flip every switch.

POP!

The lights burst to life and they are much brighter than I thought they would be. Fluorescent bulbs are installed in the ceiling which give the basement the sterile and nauseating feeling of a mental institution. The dirt and grime and ugliness on the floor comes into view. I look around and notice that the walls are covered with makeshift wallpaper made from photos, newspaper clippings, sloppily handwritten notes, and other cliché, crazy people things like:

THIS IS THE ONE.

DON'T BELIEVE IN ANYONE OR ANYTHING.

IT WAS HIM BUT IT WAS ALSO ME AND IT WAS ALSO YOU.

WHAT ELSE DO I NEED?

Empty pill bottles are scattered about a throw rug on the floor like spent shells from a machine gun. I bend over to pick one up and feel an incredible warmth from beneath the rug, like an oven. Like an oven under the floor, under the house.

I stand and read the bottle.

25

REALITALL
TAKE 2 TABLETS WHENEVER MALADJUSTMENT
OCCURS.
MAY CAUSE SEVERE DISINTEGRATION OF THE
MIND. TAKE WITH FOOD.

"Maladjustment?" I say with pause then slip the bottle into my pocket and take a gulp from the Lonely Sparrow.

There's a workbench that's covered with various tools, cigarette butts, pens, paper, empty bottles, manila folders, candy bar wrappers, a bowl stained blackish, and an old typewriter. A stuffed doll of a sad looking boy with one plastic eye sits atop of a book called *Learning to Speak Dutch for Fucking Morons*. A stack of typed pages rests next to the typewriter and one, half-typed page remains in the machine.

It says:

Kiddo,

The pages here represent all I have done. I know I was not good. I know I was not there. But it was for this. Now this is for you.

Lane Laszlo is a person who was sent to me. He was sent from It up above through the thing down below and put in me to help me investigate Everything. He helped me find my way. He helped me find my me and my peace and my happiness.

I'm a writer, boy. Like you. I've been writing a story for a long time and I need help now. I need you.

Lane Laszlo is a "fictional" character created by It and forced into my soul through the thing down below to show me the path of Everything. He was conjured by It and delivered to me through the place in the basement. I was battling depression and fighting off the effects of a time-shifting and reality-bending existence and Lane Laszlo helped me my find my path. He's a private eye and a detective and a man and he makes sense to me. He makes sense of me. He was sent as a fully formed and fully realized human and he's always ready to tackle my problems and lead the way. He can help you too, kiddo. He's here for us. For us Groffs. He's our guy. He's our good guy. Our good thing.

Let him in, kiddo.

Let him be with you, kiddo.

Let him be you, kiddo.

It's not always going to make sense, but that's okay. It's not supposed to make sense and even if it does, it doesn't. Making sense is making fiction out of fact. Remember that. Forget sense. Forget fiction. Forget fact. Remember Lane Laszlo.

Write him.

Feel him.

Love him.

I am him.

You are him.

Be him.

Best,
Dad

I raise my eyes and look at the scraps and notes and photos and chaos around me. This basement. This pit. This Hell.

I'm not whoever this Lane Laszlo is. I'm not my father. I'm not anything.

CHAPTER FIVE

Perspective

This story is about to switch from first person to third person for a bit. Then it'll switch back. And then it'll probably switch back again. And then do that a few more times.

It's going to do that because I want it to do that. Because I'm in charge of it.

I think.

CHAPTER SIX

Lane Emerges?

He was in the dark. The kind of dark that's afraid of itself. He was waiting for something but he didn't know what. He was there. Waiting. Waiting for nothing.

A door opened and light poured in and a lady called his name.
"Lane Laszlo. You're up."
He stood and followed her into an office. There was a desk and a hanging lightbulb and peeling wallpaper and it smelled like armpits and sneakers.
"Sit."

He sat by the desk and the lady plopped onto the flattened pillow on the seat of the office chair. She pulled a pencil from her puffball hairdo and pointed it toward Lane.
"PI," she said, gazing over bifocals.
"PI?" he replied.
"Dirty dick," she said with a red smirk. There was lipstick on her teeth that made Lane want to vomit.
"That's it?" he asked.
"For now."
"Do I have a girlfriend?"
"Nope."
"Hobbies?"
"Nada."
"Any identifiable personality whatsoever?"
"That's what you bring to the table, Laszlo. You know that."
Lane sighed. "What's this PI gig entail?"

She glanced to a folder on the desk, licked a finger, and flipped through some pages. With the tip of the pencil she pointed to a line.

"Uncertain at this time," she read.

"Are you kidding me?"

The lady smiled and shrugged. "What can I say? Gotta do what ya gotta do."

"Shit," he said. "Now what?"

"Get to your place and wait. Sit and wait. Maybe have a beer."

"So I should sit and wait?"

"Sit and wait. Wait and sit."

"But what about—"

"You should know the drill by now, Laszlo."

"Remind me. I love hearing you say it," he said sarcastically.

The woman tightened her mouth. "You become you. You wait for the call. The call comes. The happens happens. And that's that."

Lane sighed. "I become I."

"You become you."

"Again."

"Always."

Lane sighed another. "That it?" he said.

"That it," the lady said.

"Sit and wait," he said.

"And wait and sit, Mr. Private Investigator. Wait and sit."

CHAPTER SEVEN

The Psycho Killer Down the Street Part 2: I Gotta Get Him!

Daniel Groff Jr.
Grade 3
October 25, 1989

I lifted myself off the pavement. I went over to the Psycho to see if he was dead. I crouched next to him and he turned around and grabbed my throat. I screamed in terror. I picked up a large rock and hit him right in the head with it. He got knocked out cold. I stood up and ran away.

I went to my house because it was nearby to get some supplies. I got a butcher knife from my kitchen and a bat from my room. Then I took one of my winter gloves and took it downstairs to my garage. I took four 5" nails and stuck them through the glove right above where your fingers go. Then I took the bat and stuck five 6" nails through the top of it. I strapped the bat to my back with a belt and held the knife in my left hand and the glove on my right. I ran outside to where the Psycho was but he was gone.

I looked to my left and saw him trying to break into someone's car. I ran over to stop him. When I got there he had just got the door unlocked. I ran right up next to the car and he swung the door open and hit me right in the midsection. I fell to my knees in pain. He jumped in the car and sped away. I went searching. Then I realized where he might go.

I stood staring at his old house. They had condemned it and were just about to knock it down. They had the trucks there and everything. I quickly ran up to the house and climbed into a window. I heard him rummaging through his stuff in the next room. He seemed to be looking for something. I ran to him and stuck him with the nails in the neck. He screamed and punched me in the face and kicked me in the stomach. I threw up. He pulled out what he was looking for. It was a big machete! He swung at me and missed. I kicked him in the face and punched him in the stomach. Suddenly, a big wrecking ball came through the wall and hit him. He flew through the other wall and it just missed me because I ducked. He was gone.

The end?

CHAPTER EIGHT

Fragments

I bring my legs up Yoga-style on the stool at the workbench. I pull a smoke from the pack of Kools. I light the tip with the Zippo and puff. I don't inhale yet. I don't want to cough and choke and hack. I puff for now. I pull the pill bottle from my pocket and shake the remaining tablet like the worst maraca ever and stand it next to the pages.

"Whenever maladjustment occurs, huh?" I say to no one in particular.

I snatch up the pill bottle and dump the tablet into my hand and toss it into my mouth. I wash it down with some Lonely Sparrow and swallow it. It tastes like an M&M. I set the empty bottle next to the typewriter, remove dead-ass Uncle Double-Shirt's sunglasses from my shirt pocket, and slide them onto the face of the sad little doll with the one little eye.

"Now you're cool," I say to it.

I pick up one of the pages from the stack next to the typewriter and I'm about to read...

DING DONG

The doorbell. The door. Someone's at the door.

DING DONG

I climb under the workbench and clutch my knees to my chest.

DING DONG

I want to ignore it but I don't know how.

DING DONG DING DONG DING DONG DING DONG

I crawl out and rush up the stairs and whip open the door.

"WHAT!"

A girl. She's about 25. She's wearing a big woolen winter hat. I can see that she has purple hair that happens to be dripping wet and she has piercings in her face. She's got green eyes that look sad and I like them. She's holding a potted plant.

"Hello," she says.
"Hi."
"Who are you?"
"Who are *you*?"
"My name is Abby. I'm looking for Daniel."
"Abby?"
"Abby Abigail. Where's Daniel?"
"That's me."
"No, it's not."
"It's not?"
"No."
"Why do you say that?"
"Cuz I know him. He's not you."
"You sure?" I say.
"He's way older. Like old. As fuck. Like a man."
I stare at the plant and wonder what type it is. It's green and leafy and has blackish berries and little purple flowers that match the color of Abby's hair.

She raises it. "This is a gift for Daniel. I haven't seen him in a while and I wanted to give it to him. I heard he was sick."

"What kind of plant is it?"

She looks at it, "I don't know. I saw it at the place and it looked cool and I thought he would dig it." She looks back to me, "Ya know?"

"I guess." I say.

"Is he here?"

"Nah."

"Nah?"

"Nah."

She laughs. "Is he coming back soon?"

"Nah."

"Nah?"

"Nah."

She furrows. "Who are you?"

"I'm his son."

"No way!"

"Yes way."

"*You're* Junior?"

"My name's Daniel Groff Jr. Yeah."

"Shit!" she exclaims.

"What?"

"I heard about you, man."

"Really?"

"Yeah. Daniel told me about his kid. Said me and him would be pals."

"Why?"

"I don't know. He said that sometimes."

I take the pack of smokes from my pocket and pull one out with my teeth. I make it look natural. "Want one?" I ask, extending the pack to her.

"Sure, I guess," she says and clutches the plant in her left hand while taking a cig with her right.

I spark the Zippo with the police badge lighter and light hers, then mine. We stand there and puff. I inhale this time. I don't want her to think I'm lame.

"These are Daniel's Kools ain't they?" she says with the cigarette between her fingers.

"They're mine now."

"Cool," she says and exhales with a nod, "Cool with a C."

We puff some more and stand and let the world be for a bit. It feels weird.

"Did you just get out of the shower or something?" I ask her.

She shrugs and it annoys me.

"Okay," I say.

"Well," she says after a beat, "I don't really have anything to talk to you about. When Daniel comes back, whenever that is, give him this. Okay?"

She hands me the plant.

"Okay," I say.

"Cool."

"With a C," I say.

She smiles. "Thanks for the cigarette," she says and hands me the burning butt. "Maybe I'll come back soon and we can smoke some more and maybe go for a walk or something."

"Yeah, I guess we can do that."

"Maybe we can get drunk or something too. Ya know?"

"We'll see."

"Cool. See ya later, Daniel Jr."

"Bye, Abby."

I walk inside and Abby doesn't move. She stands there and closes her eyes and sniffs the air and smiles. And I close the door in her face.

I notice a note that sits next to the D I drew on the dusty old desk:

DEAR DANIEL,

I'M SORRY BUT I CAN'T DO THIS ANYMORE. I HAVE TO GO.

SINCERELY,
MOM

I look toward the kitchen and realize that I've forgotten about Mom. But I guess she left. She'll be fine.

I open the top drawer of the desk to put the note inside and find a similar piece of paper, though it's yellowed and curled. It sits next to a gold wedding band. The note says:

DEAR DANIEL,

I'M SORRY BUT I CAN'T DO THIS ANYMORE. I
HAVE TO GO.

SINCERELY,
MIA

I place both notes in the drawer and bring the plant
downstairs and put it next to the typewriter.

I put Abby's cigarette in my mouth alongside my own and puff
them both simultaneously. I can taste her spit. It tastes good.
Abby's cute and I think I like her. I hope she comes back later.

I hope we get drunk and I hope we laugh. Maybe when she
comes back some kind of happiness will come with her. Not sure
why I think that would happen, but I do. I think it can follow her
into my new house like a lost dog. Happiness and something and
that sort of thing. That sort of thing is the good sort of thing. The
good sort of thing is the sort of thing that I need.

Right?

I don't know. I don't know what the right feelings are.

So I take another drink.

CHAPTER NINE

The Psycho Killer Down the Street Part 3: Psycho Killer in My School!

Daniel Groff Jr.
Grade 3
November 8, 1989

One school day I was in art class. Our teacher was showing us her favorite art. She said it was a Rothko. She bought it from a museum for $85,000. Then suddenly all the lights in the school went out and I heard Mrs. Martin scream. I ran to the light switch and turned on the lights. I saw Mrs. Martin laying on her desk bleeding! I ran over to see if she was okay. I checked her pulse but as soon as I touched her throat she rolled off her desk onto her stomach and I saw something familiar, a knife with PSYCHO scratched into the blade was sticking out of her back.

"Oh no, there's only one person who's got a knife like that. That Psycho is back and in my school! He's getting really annoying now! I killed him three stupid times already. Well, now I gotta go find him and get the crap kicked out of me."

Suddenly the lights went out again.
Bang! A gun shot.
It hit me in the shoulder. I was hurt bad. Then I heard someone running. I listened carefully and ran to where I heard the sound. I saw him. I ran really fast and caught him. I dove on him. He grabbed a steel chair and smashed it in my face. I was bleeding bad. He got up and kicked me hard in my stomach. He punched me twice in the face and smashed me through a

window. He came outside and smashed me back through another window. We were back inside he threw me against the wall HARD! He smashed me against the floor and kicked me again. He pulled his knife and stuck it through my hand and nailed my hand to the ground. He took out his gun and pressed it against my head. I had to do something. I took a freshly sharpened pencil and stabbed it through his eye. He screamed and ran. He was gone. An ambulance came and picked me up. It was over.

The end?

CHAPTER TEN
Atropine

When Abby came back, I let her in and we went into the basement and sat on the floor and smoked the last few cigarettes.

She brought some hamburgers from a fast food restaurant but I refused to eat those because I recently decided to become a vegetarian and I only eat organic, natural foods and use organic, natural soaps. The soaps smell like dirt and hippies. She got offended but I don't care. My health is important to me.

She also brought a flask with something in it and we traded it back-and-forth. We swigged and slurped and got a little silly, which made me want to get a lot silly.

With her.

With her, I want to get silly.

"Your pop still ain't back, huh?" she asked.
"Not yet."
"That sucks."
"I guess."
"He's a pretty cool guy."
"Oh yeah?"
"Yeah."
"That's weird."
"Why?"
"I don't know. Just is. Dads. Ya know?"

She takes a drag, "Whatever."

"How do you know him anyway?"

"Secret."

"Seriously?"

"Seriously secretive secrets, yo," she says

"Okay."

She tousles my hair. "I'll tell you later!"

I smile.

"What do you wanna do, Danny?"

I shrug.

"Can I call you Danny?"

I shrug again.

"Senior hated it."

"He hated pork chops too."

She falls on her back and locks her fingers behind her head like she's about to do crunches, "Danny it is!"

"Danny it is," I say and lie next to her and lock my fingers behind my head, like her.

She looks at me and giggles, "So?"

I shrug a fourth time. I'm supposed to climb on top of her and kiss her now. But I don't do it.

"What do you do for fun?" she asks.

"I don't know. Nothing, I guess."

"Sounds like a hoot."

I have nothing to say to that.

"Do you like drugs?" she says.

"I've never done them. Well, I took a pill. And I drink." I take another gulp.

She smiles. "You know that plant I brought?"

I look at the potted plant on the workbench, "Yeah."

"You know what it is?"

"No."

"It's called Atropa Belladonna. Do you know what that is?"

"No."

She smiles and pauses and squints and I'm nervous. "Can I tell you something?" she asks.

"Sure," I say.

She sits up. I do too. She grabs my arms and drags me closer to her. "I like you," she says.

Our knees touch. It's like an electric shock to my balls and I want her. I kiss her and push my tongue between her lips. But she gets up and walks away.

She wipes my slobber from her mouth with the back of her hand. "Do you know what your dad was doing before he died?" she asks while looking at my spit as if she expects it to be green.

The embarrassment is put on hold. "Wait. You know he's dead?"

She nods.

"Why did you say you didn't?"

She shrugs. "Do you know what he was doing?"

"He was writing something."

"Yeah, you know what?"

"Some book about something."

"It was a detective story about this guy…"

"Lane Laszlo?"

"That's the one."

"It's pretty much the most important thing ever written by anything and it's going to change everything."

"Okay."

"Everything with a capital E."

"Isn't that a little dramatic?"

"It sounds like it is, but it isn't. Believe me. Seriously. It's legit," she says.

I don't buy this shit one bit.

She continues, "Do you know what samizdat is?"

"No."

"Like, underground books."

"Okay."

"Manifestos. Illegal books that were passed around by hand. Grassroots. They're a way to get the message out when the man didn't want the message out."

"Okay."

"Soviet shit. Commies, ya know?"

"Okay."

"Your pop was working on this book about Lane Laszlo and it was gonna be like big and shit. Down and dirty, but on the down low, ya know? Down low and dirty. To avoid censorship."

"Censorship from the man?" I say.

"Censorship from the self!" She pulls the flask and unscrews the cap and drinks and swallows. "Our biggest enemy is us, man. Us is the man, man," she says as she approaches and hands me the drink. "We're killing us."

I drink to my confusion. This all sounds so Intro-to-something college class-y. And it sounds stupid. And lame.

"We have potential. We have possibility. We have power. But we don't let us take advantage of it. We constantly get in our way. We constantly fight us. We constantly destroy us."

"But we're us. Aren't we?" I ask.

She snatches the flask. "We're not *only* us."

"What do you mean?"

"We all belong to one thing. One thing that everything belongs to. All of us make up everything which makes up Everything, which makes up us, which makes up Everything. And we're killing It," she says. "We're the virus, but we're the cure. We're the vaccine, but we're the disease. We're the body *and* we're the soul. We're the environment. We're the pollution. We're the violence. We're the love. We're the hate. We're the sex. We're the fucking. We're the Everything, Danny. The Everything is us. Everything with a capital E."

"Abby, what exactly do you—"

"And the Everything is broken."

"How is it broken?"

"It is."

"That's not a very good answer."

"Well, it is," she says and looks to her sneakers. "There's a river running beneath our feet. Don't you feel it? Don't you hear it? Don't you smell it?"

I look to her feet and back to her face, "No."

She grimaces, "You will. Once you write it. Once you read it. You will."

"Write what?"

"Your dad's work. The book. *Lane Laszlo and the Broken Everything*. That's the title. You're here to finish it. That's why you're *here*," she says, pointing to the floor. "You're here to finish his shit. You're here to live his shit. You're here to discover and to learn and to love and to be the him. The new him. The new him that we're all gonna love a lot. The new him that we're all gonna love as much as the other him. The other him is gone but that doesn't mean he's *gone*. The Everything needs to be fixed. Because Everything feeds from Everything feeds from Everything feeds from Everything. So it's pretty important to make sure that works, right?"

Deep inhale time, "I'm supposed to finish writing his book."

"Yes."

"But what if I don't want to?" I say.

"You're a writer," she says.

"So?"

"So was he."

"So?"

She sighs. "We're the result of the decisions and the choices and the randomness and the chaos of every person who came before us and every person who came before them and every person who came before them, and so on and so on and so on."

"Okay..."

"For like, zillions of years."

"Zillions?" I say.

"And if some dude in the 1400s makes a left instead of a right, you're never born. You know what I mean?" she says.

"I think so." I say.

"And if you're never born, I'm not here right now, and that means I'm doing something else like getting in a car crash, or eating pizza, or petting a dog, or whatever."

"Right."

"So your existence changes shit. It changes people's lives. Even if you don't realize it. That's how important you are. That's how important we all are," she says.

"I see."

"That's how important everything is. That's how important *the* Everything is."

"Everything with a capital E?"

"Yes!"

"But what does this have to do with writing some book?"

She sighs again and casually pulls a few berries from the plant on the bench and holds them to me. "Eat these."

"What?"

"Eat these berries."

I look at them. "Why?"

"Because I'm telling you to."

"I don't want to eat those berries."

"Eat the fucking berries, Danny."

"Why?"

"Because the berries are important."

"What do they do?"

"Things."

"What kind of things?" I say.

She grunts. "Stop asking questions."

"No?"

She pauses and sucks down the rage. "Eat the berries."

"No," I say.

"Eat. The fucking. Berries!"

"NO!"

She grabs my tie and pulls me to my feet and forces my back into the workbench, pressing against me.

"I need you to eat this shit," she says within an inch me.

"Abby, you're making me incredibly uncomfortable. My hands are starting to sweat."

"I don't care about your fucking hands."

"There are feelings that I'm feeling right now, and I don't like them one bit."

She breathes measured breaths from her nose, in and out and in and out and in and out as she stares at me with disgust. "I'm gonna kiss you now," she says.

"Okay," I say.

And she places one hand and one berry-filled fist on the sides on my face and gently leans her lips into mine and swirls her tongue against mine and breathes harder and harder and I grab handfuls of her hair. We breathe, but not in unison, and that distracts me and I forget to move my tongue and I can feel her frustration through my face. And she grunts, pushing me backward until I'm sitting on the workbench and she climbs up and straddles me and kisses me harder. And I remember to move my tongue now as she pushes herself into me and I can feel her and she can feel me and we move together and she pushes more into me, and more into me, and more into me. And I feel her warmth, and it's heating up, and it hurts a little, and there's something I dislike. And she opens her mouth wider and I feel her teeth on my lip and she pushes me down. And she kisses my neck and loosens my tie and rips open my shirt and ruins my shirt and kisses my chest. And I think about my shirt and I feel things under my back and I want her bad and I want this to stop and I want to be more comfortable but this is what passion is and I go with it because this is what you do because even if you hate what you're doing. You do it because the idea of this passion is what you're going for. It's not the real passion and it's not the real love and it's not the real feeling, it's the idea. And the idea wins.

And somehow my pants are off and her pants are off and we're moving together and I feel all of her as she pulls both her shirt and bra off at the same time. And I'm angry because I wanted to see her bra. But I touch her and move my hands on her and her skin feels good and she still has those berries in her fist and I'm wondering when she's going to try to make me eat them. And I'm distracted by the berries now. And now would be a good time to try because I feel good and I'd do whatever she wanted because I feel me in her and her on me and we move and she's wet and she's making sounds and I can't tell if they're real but there's some sweat on her lower back and I want to taste it. And I want to step away and watch us and can't wait for this to be over and her to be gone so I can remember it later when I'm jerking off and I can have this memory of this thing and this stuff and remember these feelings as feelings. And she moves faster and I move faster and she screams and it makes me uncomfortable but I go with it because that's what you do because the screaming is part of the idea. And I think about screaming too but I don't have to scream. But I do have to finish and I move faster and she moves faster and she screams louder and I grab her hips and squeeze and everything happens the way it happens and it feels good. And I shouldn't have done it where I did it but I did it and now it's done.

And she puts the berries in my hand and I eat them.

"Thank you," she says.

She climbs off me and the bench, finds her bra and pants, and puts them both on. She sits on the warm rug on floor and sips on the flask. "I think I'm drunk now," she says.

I stand, pull on my pants, take the flask, drink, and wince on the swallow. "Me too," I say.

She closes her eyes and rubs her temples. "Let's wait a bit till those fuckers kick in, okay?"

"Are you okay?" I ask.

"I think I feel a migraine coming on." She pats the floor next to her, "Sit here with me."

I do.

I pass the flask and she grabs it, knocks it back, and passes it to me.

"I'm not trying to hurt you," she says.

"Okay," I say.

"There's this shit, this shit that I know and this shit that I understand, and I got this need and pull and drive to tell it to you."

"What do you mean?"

"I know that you need information and I know that I got information. That's it."

And things start feeling weird.

"How does finishing a book fix The Everything?" I say as the world blurs like I opened my eyes underwater.

"You gotta find the authentic truth. The universal truth. The unifying truth," she says.

And things starts feeling weirder.

"No biggie, right?" she says with a knowing smirk.

And I swill the shit big time on the pass-back and almost barf it back out.

"You're vague, Abby. You're like a mysterious mystery maker

or something. Mysterious mysteries abound or some shit!"

She shrugs, "That's the way it is, Danny."

I'm not sure what to say to that and I don't say nothing. I sit and I wait wait wait.

"Feel anything yet?" she asks.

I shake my bake. "I don't think... No. I feel the fuzzies from the boozies but not much else else, ya know? Ya know?"

She grins and nods.

"What's the funniest funnies, bunny buddy?" I sort of say.

She shruggy shrug, "Talkin' funny is all."

Let laugh. "Shiiiiiit. Shake a tail at that mess and I'll lay you deep once more!" I blip in her mug.

"Fiction's got ya, Danny. Fiction's got ya, big time," she slips up and down on the fadeaway slideroll.

"Fiction got YA!" I yarlp at the backway.

"Goin... goin... gone, Mr. Laszlo!" out her motorway.

And the driftin' and the sailin' and the always always on the one way.

"Let's get you to the typerwriterererer..." she make with the make make.

And that's it for the that it.

And that it.

And up and she pulls away.

Up and she pulls away and I go and I go and I go.

And black. And back. And Everything. And

CHAPTER ELEVEN

GBU

Eggs. Black coffee. Half a grapefruit. He popped the toast before it was done because he was sick of waiting. He was already waiting. Why wait for more, he thought. He buttered the half-toasted bread and plopped in the old recliner and flipped on the tube. *The Good, the Bad and the Ugly* was on. He smiled and settled in.

He knocked back a sip and winced from the craziness. It was strong and it was brutal and he needed it like that. He swallowed it down and sighed. Relaxed. Calm. Cool. Collected.

He sopped some yolk with a folded half of half-toast and jammed the dripping yellow into his mouth. It tasted good and greasy and fattening. He took another sip and looked into Clint Eastwood's cowboy eyes. He looked into those weathered, leathered peepers and saw what the world could do to a man. He saw the strength in silence and the resolve in stillness. He saw this man, this man with no name and smiled. Life was good. Life was right. Life was fine.

And then the call came.

"What do I gotta do?" Lane asked after grabbing the receiver.
"What you do," the man on the phone said.
"And what's that?"
"What you need."
"Should I even ask for details?"

"You'll get your imperatives."

"Oh good, my *imperatives*," Lane said while mimicking a jack off.

"Don't sass me."

"*Sass* you?"

"Sass me. Don't do it."

"Yikes," Lane said and took a breath. "What is it? Missing person? Cheating fuckface? Murder?"

"You know I don't know."

"Yeah, yeah, yeah, I know you don't know nothing."

"Right," the man said.

"What do I do then?"

"I don't know. Wait, I guess."

"Lots of waiting, eh?"

"You in or not?" the man said.

There was a pause as Lane watched the stand-off. Clint watching Van Cleef watching Wallach watching Van Cleef watching Clint watching Wallach. Eyes, hands, guns. Good, bad, ugly.

"Still there?" the man asked.

"Yeah, I'm here. Is that it?"

"Basically. Sending over the imperatives now."

Lane stood and carried the phone over the to the small, ancient, coffee-teeth-stained printer in the corner. He waited as the machine spewed forth a long, ticker tape-like piece of paper. He cradled the receiver between his head and shoulder and ripped the paper from the tiny beast's mouth.

He read:

THE FICTION IS NOT WHAT THIS IS / THE REAL IS NOT THE FICTION THAT THIS IS / AND IF YOU CHANGE THEN THE CHANGE IS WHAT THIS IS / THERE IS A RIVER RUNNING BENEATH OUR FEET AND WE KNOW YOU CAN FEEL IT / YOU WILL GO TO 7 MILBERG PLACE AND MAKE THIS WHAT IT IS / INVESTIGATE NOTHING / PLEASE? / PLEASE / YES? / YES / THANK YOU / YOU'RE WELCOME

"What's this job pay?" he said on his way back to the recliner.

"What do you think?"

"Lots?"

"Yeah right."

"Nothing?"

"Nothing," the man said.

"Hmm, I'm shocked," Lane said.

"Bigger picture. You know how it is, Laszlo."

"Do I?"

"I hope so."

Lane sat down and finished off the joe. He glanced at the flick and wished he had a cigar like Clint's. "Who is this, by the way?" Lane said.

"I work for It," he said. "Don't sweat it too much, kiddo. That's not your job."

"Mm," Lane said and stared at the TV.

"What are you doing, Lane?" the man said.

"Watching a movie," Lane said.

"Which one?"

"Like you don't know."

"I don't."

"Bullshit."

"Really, I have no idea."

Lane turned and looked back to the security camera near the ceiling. He saw the flashing red light that told him this man who worked for It was watching. It. Whatever the fuck It was. It was always gawking at Lane like some perverted creep. Like some weirdo. This was Lane's life. This was all he knew. He could only question It to the point of questioning It. Anything further was impossible. Everything was always to be accepted.

He smirked and shook his head and waved.

"I can see you," he said.

"But I can't see you, not right now," the man said.

"You in the shitter or something?"

"No, I'm not watching right now is all. It's not an all the time thing, ya know. I've got something in line."

"I don't buy it."

"Bigger fish sometimes, Laszlo. You ain't the only one swimming."

Lane felt strangely insulted. Which made him feel strangely uncomfortable. Which led to an awkward silence that stiffened the muscles in his neck.

"Listen, Laszlo," the man said, "All I know is that you're being called up. I know that you're going to work. And I know you're gonna feel a little different for a while. But It told me you'd help. It told me the way."

"How's this time gonna be different?"

"Don't know."

"Will *I* know?"

"Can't tell you."

"Well, what am I supposed to do?"

"You're an investigator, Laszlo. Investigate."

"I'm not an investigator." Lane said.

"C'mon, Lane," the man said. " You know what you gotta do to solve this fuckin' thing."

"I do?"

"Yes. So do it."

Lane sighed and sat for a long one as he turned to the movie and watched the Good put a bullet in the Bad.

"Okay," he said as Van Cleef's bad body rolled into the grave of the Unknown. "I'll do what I gotta do."

"Atta boy," the man said.

And they hung up.

As the Good and the Ugly stood at the grave of the Unknown, Lane kept on watching.

CHAPTER TWELVE

The Psycho Killer Down the Street Part 4: The End of the Psycho?

Daniel Groff Jr.
Grade 3
November 22, 1989

I was riding in the ambulance and the sirens were blaring. It was scary in there. But I knew I had to go to the hospital. I was hurt very bad. Suddenly the ambulance started skidding all over the place. Then I heard the two paramedics scream. I stood up and looked out the window and I saw the two guys fly out the doors. I was frightened and was wondering who threw those guys.

Suddenly, the truck stopped. Then I heard footsteps coming back towards me. He jumped at me. I felt a sudden sting in my leg and I started getting woozy. I fell asleep. He injected me with a sleeping liquid.

I was asleep for about two hours. I awoke. I opened my eyes to see that nut The Psycho Killer driving. I got up very quietly and went to the window. I looked out and all I saw was country. I guessed we were in Upstate New York. The ambulance stopped and I heard the guy saying, "I better go and check the little idiot."

I ran to the bed and pretended that I was still asleep. He took a bottle of smelling salts and put it under my nose. I opened my eyes in a jolt. Then the guy said, "You little idiot. I'm gonna kill you as soon as we get to my farm." I had to do something, but what? I grabbed a scalpel and cut part of his ear off!

"Ahhhh," he screamed. "You jerk. I'll kill you now!" I kicked him in the stomach and punched him in the face. He punched me and I tripped over a first-aid kit and hit the shift in the front of the truck into neutral. The truck started rolling down a hill. He jumped at me and hit my head against the dashboard. He smashed me through a window and threw me out. He thought I was dead but I held onto the door. I pulled myself up and grabbed him by the throat and said, "If I'm going, you're coming with me!"

Then the truck flipped off a cliff. I prepared to die when a blue light surrounded me and I was taken to Heaven. I heard a voice, it must've been God. He said he needs me for another great adventure and should I choose to accept it, it will be my most challenging ever. I would have to stop Satan and Hell from taking over Earth. I said I accept. Suddenly everything got black. I awoke sitting in my backyard.

The end?

Part Two

CHAPTER THIRTEEN

Twilight Sleep

"You kicked me again," she says.

She?

"Between you and him, I'm never going to get any sleep."

Abby. She's sitting up in bed wearing a bathrobe and a towel tied around her head. She turns to me, smiles, and eyes me with eyes that understand why I'm lying in bed next to her.

"What was with the screaming?" she says, "It was getting scary."

"Abby?" I say.

"Mm hm," she yawns.

"Whose bed is this?"

"What?"

"Whose bed is this? Is this my dad's bed?"

"What are you talking about?"

"Is this my dad's bed? Am I just now coming around from those things you made me eat?"

"What things?"

"The berries. Those things you gave me. Those things that made me trip my face off."

She looks worried. What did I say? Why is she confused?

I sit up. "The berries, Abby! The berries you made me eat after you fucked me in my father's basement. Remember?"

Her eyes narrow. "Why are you making such a big deal about

berries right now?"

"What do you mean?"

"That was a long time ago. What made you think about that?"

"What made me think about that?"

"Yeah."

"It happened like 10 minutes ago!"

"What?"

"It just fucking happened, Abby! It fucked my head like 10 minutes ago!"

"Wait..."

"Why are you acting all—"

"Slow down..."

"Seriously, what's the fucking deal?"

"Danny, that happened months ago."

Bullshit. "Bullshit."

She touches my head, "Are you okay?"

I slap her hand away.

"What's your problem?" she asks.

"Why are you fucking with me?"

"I'm not."

I look around the room. Clothes are strewn about and strange pictures hang on walls. This place is lived-in. And not lived-in the way that my dad lived in it. It's lived-in by new people. Us people.

"What is this?" I ask.

"You're starting to scare me," she says as she slowly sits up. And I see it. Her belly. Her big, round belly that can only be filled with one thing.

And I'm out of the bed.

"What the fuck?" I shout.

"What's the matter with you?"

"Tell me what's going on, or I'm gonna lose it! I swear to fucking god—"

And I see tears have filled her eyes as she stares at my clenched fist. My clenched fist that seems to have a mind of its own. My clenched fist that I was about to use whether I thought it was right or wrong.

"How can I tell you when I don't understand you?" she says through welling tears.

I breathe a few, unclench, and lower my hand. "I'm feeling confused," I say.

"Come sit down," she says, patting the bed.

I sit and she rests a hand on my leg. "Now, tell me what's going on."

"I don't know. I remember being in the basement, and then I remember the berries, and then I was having these dreams. And now... I don't know."

"I think you might've overdone it last night," she says motioning toward the nightstand. I look and see an empty bottle of whiskey and at least a half-dozen empty beer bottles.

"I drank that?"

She nods.

"Did you have any?"

"Hello?" she says and points to her gigantic belly.

I place my hand on the mound and hold it there. It feels wrong but it feels right. Like it is what it is. I can't explain it any further than that. She covers my hand with her own and I notice a gold wedding band is around her left ring finger. It's a ring that looks familiar.

Is it possible that I simply drank myself stupid and forgot months of time? Is it possible that I missed whatever this all is? Is it possible to not notice this? Do I have a fucking brain tumor?

"I guess my head is fucked this morning," I say. "I'm sorry I lost my temper. It won't ever happen again."

She grins and nods a knowing nod that tells me that she's heard this line before. And I don't know what to say, so I say what I think I'm supposed to say. "I love you, Abby."

And she places a hand on my face.

"Go downstairs and work for a while. I'll make us eggs."

I nod and she slowly climbs out of bed, holding her belly like it could drop and hit the floor.

"There's aspirin in the bathroom, I think. If you didn't finish it yesterday," she says without looking back.

And I stay. In my bed? In my house? In my life?

I stay.

CHAPTER FOURTEEN

I.

Things were tough for Lane Laszlo. He'd been on the job for only a few hours and it had already gotten old as hell. He sat in his '82 Volvo and stared at the front of the house at 7 Milberg Place. Nothing happened. The house looked nice. Suburban. Peaceful. Sensible. Nice lawn. Usual shit.

What was he supposed to be doing? Was somebody going to come here and do something strange or threatening or seedy or whatever? He had no idea. It told him to come here, so he came here, and that was it.

"How the fuck am I supposed to be a PI If I don't know what I'm supposed to I.?" he said and stared for another few beats. "Fuck it, I'm going in." He stepped out of the car.

As he walked across the front lawn and approached the door he felt a tension grab him. A change in atmosphere, like he wandered into a patch of humidity. "Something bad," he thought. "Something bad, something bad, something bad."

But he knocked anyway.

"LANE!" a middle-aged woman said when she spotted the newly christened private eye after opening the door. She held a pair of gardening shears in one gloved-hand and a bundle of some kind of green leaves with purple flowers and berries in the other. "I was hoping you'd stop by."

"Do I know you?" Lane asked.

"No," she said. "No, you don't." She set the shears onto a table next to the door, pulled a glove off her right hand, and went for the shake, "I'm Abby."

Lane took her hand.

"I'm part of this whole thing," she said with a warm smile.
"Part of what whole thing?" he said.
She smiled again. "Come on inside. I made some coffee."

Lane stepped through the door and immediately moved from scary-humid-land to I-feel-kinda-okay-land. The house was good. It was right. It felt like a home.

"How do you take it?" Abby asked on her way into the kitchen.

"Black," Lane said. He checked out the framed photos hanging on the walls. Most were of some desperate looking kid posing in various settings: a zoo, a park, a backyard. A few featured a much younger, punky-looking Abby standing next to a scruffy guy with shaggy hair and a beat up suit.

Abby returned, handing Lane a mug that showed a dead cartoon cat hanging from a noose around its neck exclaiming, "Hang in there, kiddo!"

"Piping hot cuppa black," she said with that same warmth as before.

"Thanks," Lane said. He tried to sip from his mug, but the steaming liquid nearly burned his lips off.

She glanced at the photo of the man with the younger version of herself on the wall and her demeanor cooled. "Want to sit down, Lane?" she said.

Lane nodded and followed her into the living room.

"So, as I said, I was hoping you'd stop by."

"Why is that?" Lane said.

"Sit," she said, motioning to the puffy white sofa.

Lane sat.

"I don't know why," she said and sat on the love seat adjacent to the sofa, "but sometimes I think about you and I say, 'Boy, I hope Lane stops by.'"

Lane stared uncomfortably, unsure how to react.

Abby smiled, "You almost never do."

"Almost?" he said.

"Well," she took a sip from her coffee, "you're here now."

Lane chuckled, "Right. So what does 'you're involved in this whole thing,' mean exactly?"

Abby shrugged, "I don't know. I mean, I know, but I don't know."

After an awkward beat they both laughed.

"I guess it's all pretty peculiar," she said.

"Do you know what I do, Abby?" Lane said.

"You're a private eye."

"And how do you know that?"

Abby shrugged.

"Because I just found out myself."

"That's odd."

"Sure is," Lane said.

They each stared; Lane toward the floor, Abby toward Lane.

She took a breath. "Sometimes, I think about the river beneath our feet," she said without moving her eyes. "Sometimes I think about where we are. Where we're going. Where we'll be. Where we came from." She shifted her gaze to Lane. "Sometimes I think about what put us here. What made us. All of the choices and randomness and messiness and meaninglessness. All of it. Sometimes I think about those things, and those things lead me to you." She leaned forward, "You're something to me, Lane. You're floating in my river with me. You're here, and I'm not alone." She reached out and touched his knee with her fingertips. "You're what I know," she said, "and that's good."

Lane shot her hand a look, "But, what does that mean, Abby?"

Abby pulled back, "I don't even know what I'm talking about. I don't know anything about this stuff." She rested her hand on the side of her mug. "But I *do* know, it doesn't really matter."

"What doesn't?" Lane said.

"It," she said with a shrug.

"There sure is a lot of shrugging involved in this, isn't there?" Lane said.

She smirked and shrugged again.

Lane placed his mug on a coaster on the end table next to the couch. "Do you have something for me to investigate? Some kind of cheating husband thing? Some kind of missing person thing? A bad business partner? Anything? Anything at all?" he said.

Abby tightened her mouth, which Lane registered as disappointment, and he couldn't help but feel guilty about that. "Would that make it easier for you?" she said.

"Yes," he said.

She sighed, stood, and walked into the other room.

Lane sat and stewed in his discomfort. He was already sick of this private eye business. Was it always this cryptic? Phillip Marlowe's cases didn't always make sense, but at least some sultry dame slinked into his office and told him what was what. Lane didn't have a dame. He had some pleasant, middle-aged lady with a penchant for gardening who spoke like a bottle of Dr. Bronner's soap (which he needed to pick up on the way home, by the way).

When Abby came back she was a holding a manila folder and her nose was bleeding.

"I hope this helps you, Lane," she said with the folder extended to him.

"Abby," Lane said abruptly, "your nose..." he said, pointing to her face.

She reached up and touched the red stuff. As she examined her crimson fingertips, her eyes drifted to Lane and melted into a mix of sadness and confusion, "Why did you do this me?" she said.

"What?" Lane said.

"I thought this was over. I thought you said..." she threw the folder and stormed into the other room.

Lane leapt to his feet. "Abby, I don't know what you think I did, but I didn't—"

She came back with a suitcase. "Take your shit and get the fuck out of here, you animal!"

Lane noticed that a badly bruised cheek had joined the blood dripping from her nostril. "I didn't do anything!" he said.

"I don't know what I do to deserve this! I don't know why you have to make me suffer like this! What did I do? Aren't I good? Don't I treat you right?"

"Abby, I don't think this—"

"Get the fuck out of here!" she screamed and flung the suitcase at him.

Lane dodged it and went for the door as Abby collapsed onto the floor.

"I'm sorry if you think I did what I you think I did," he said. "But I didn't."

"Save it, you filthy piece of shit! I'm sick of this!"

Lane started back to her with his arms outreached, "Can I please help—"

"GET THE FUCK OUT OF HERE BEFORE I CALL THE POLICE!" she screeched with all she had inside herself.

Lane wasn't equipped to deal with any of this. Lane wasn't equipped to deal with any of anything. Up until today, Lane was living a different life. He had been a bartender, a school teacher, a door-to-door salesman, a lifeguard, and even a magician. He barely remembered those lives, but he knew they were part of him. He knew he lived them even if it didn't feel like he lived them. Lane's lives felt like echoes. Like shadows. Like the stars a guy sees when he stands up too fast from lying face down on the floor all day.

But this private investigation thing felt new. Especially being assigned to a case that was as half-assed as this one.

Lane wanted out of this gig. But it going tits up, this fast, certainly intrigued him. Must be something to this shit show, he thought. He knew there had to be an answer, but the troubling part of this was, he first had to find out the question.

Lane snatched the folder from the floor, headed for the door, and left.

CHAPTER FIFTEEN

The Psycho Killer Down the Street Part 5: The Flames of Hell

Daniel Groff Jr.
Grade 3
December 6, 1989

I had to find Satan and destroy him and Hell below. But I wondered how. Suddenly the ground opened. I fell down a huge hole. "Ahhh!" I screamed.

BOOM! I hit the ground. I cut my head open. I got up and got nailed by a bunch of black demons. They picked me up and carried me to their leader, The King of Darkness himself, Satan. The demons dropped me and I hit the ground. Satan pointed his finger at me and I was lifted up. Satan stood 8 feet tall and he was bulging with muscles everywhere. He had huge fangs dripping with blood, guts, and drool. He had big yellow eyes and big horns. He was terrifying. Then he spoke, "The reason I brought you here is because you are my enemy. You're trying to destroy my workers and my home. I could squash you like a fly but I won't. Not yet at least."

I said, "Why not?"

"Because we are the same you and I. We are a team," he said.

I said, "Go bite yourself, Satan! I ain't on no team with you!"

"Then so be it," Satan said.

Suddenly I was back in my backyard. Then lightning struck and I saw the most frightening face. "Oh my God, it's you! The Psycho Killer Down the Street! I killed you three times!"

The Psycho charged at me and I kicked him in the face and he fell. I dove at him but missed. He picked me up and slammed my head against a rock. I was bleeding bad. I kicked him in the stomach and punched him in the face. He fell. I said, "You will soon be dead forever, Psycho Killer Down the Street!"

He picked me up and threw me through a glass window. I had a big piece of glass in my leg. He charged me once again. I pulled the glass out of my leg and stabbed him in the head. He disappeared.

The end?

CHAPTER SIXTEEN
The River

In the basement, at the typewriter, I read many pages and have no idea what I'm looking at. Fits and starts and things about Lane Laszlo and his pointless "investigation" into something. Words. Words and lists and nonsense and words.

Like this:

1. GIVE DEPTH TO THE DILEMMA

2. WHICH IS THE EVERYTHING?

3. EVERY SOUL IS A FRAGMENT OF A FRAGMENT OF A FRAGMENT

4. LONELY SPARROWS!

5. THE CONFABULATIONS OF...

6. THE EVERYTHING IS IT

7. WHAT IS THIS FUCKING MECHANISM OF DEATH?

8. PEOPLE WHO TAP INTO THIS "BOX" BECOME CARRIERS FOR "LOST" SOULS

9. FACILITATION OF THE COMING OF THE

EVERYTHING-EVERYTHING

10. IS THE BERRY?

11. LANE

12. LASZLO

13. BLIGHTED LANES

14. BLIGHTED BRAINS

15. ATROPINE IS GOOD

16. WHAT (WHY) DID HE (WE) DO (THAT) TO ABBY (MIA)?

Stupid words. Words with no meaning. Words that must've originated somewhere. But where? Where is the place of the words? And who runs it? Who did this? Did I do this? Did he do this? Did we do this?

And if so, why would we do this?

I don't know Lane Laszlo. There was me before, and I was all that mattered, but now there's Lane Laszlo. And he's something else and he complicates things. He complicates my life. He complicates my dreams. These things are brutalizing my consciousness. My consciousness is fragile. My consciousness is busted. I have nothing to rely on. I have nothing to set me straight.

I don't remember what's happening right now. Everything is a blur of nonsense. I'm not typing this because I can't remember doing it. I'll remember it when it becomes the past but while it's happening, I can't remember it. I have no memory of now. I only know then. Now is not now. Now is nothing. Now is only something when now becomes then. I'm disintegrating. I'm disintegrating while I type. I'm disintegrating while I breathe.

What am I feeling? What am I? Who am I? Why am I?

A broken everything, always burning, that's the inside I know. That's the inside that exists outside of time. Externally, I don't exist in the present. Not anymore. There's a time fluctuation that occurs around me. I'm bombarded with things from other places and other times and I can't exist in the present. I'm in a constant state of flux. But internally, I'm here. Outside my face the world is a throbbing mess of ugliness. But inside, nothing new ever occurs. Inside, there are only things that I already know. To learn and to live and to exist is to allow the outside in. But to me, the outside is in another time. To me, the past and the future are twirling and colliding and dancing and drooling and not letting me know the plans for my head. But I'm writing this. Even if I don't know that it's happening as it's happening it's happening. I'm writing this. The way he was writing this. The way someone else will be writing this. The way someone else after that someone else will be writing this. The way someone else after that someone else will be writing this. The way it's supposed to happen. The only way I know.

But how do I know? And what's the fucking point?

"The point is that there is no point, Danny," Abby says as she steps down the basement stairs holding a plate of eggs, toast, and a half a grapefruit in one hand and a mug in the other. "The point is, you're writing. You're working. You're making things happen. You're doing what you're here to do."

My eyes are on the pages. "But this is dumb," I say with disgust.

Abby places the plate on the desk and I see the toast is coated with jam that's a familiar shade of blackish. She sets the steaming mug of coffee next to it. A dead cat with a noose around its neck is on the mug and it's screaming, "Hang in there, kiddo!"

She rests her hand on my shoulder. "Dumb isn't important," she says and leans in close to look at the page. I can smell her hair and I feel a pain in my chest. A feeling. A good feeling? I don't know. "Done is all that matters, not dumb," she says.

I take a bite from the toast. "Well, that's dumb," I say through a mouthful.

"How's that coming by the way?"

"What, being dumb? I'm doing pretty good."

She turns to me and smiles, "I know that. I mean the done. Getting closer?"

"How am I supposed to know? I don't even remember writing any of this stuff. It could almost be done. Or it could be in the middle. I have no idea."

She straightens with a groan and her belly stares me in the face, "Why don't you go downstairs for a bit?" she says.

"Downstairs?" I say. "But we're in the basement."

She laughs through her nose, turns from me, bends down, and yanks away the throw rug from the floor revealing a wooden trap door. "Sit by the river," she says. "Watch it flow. It's relaxing."

I look from the door on the floor to my pregnant wife(?), and shoot her a quizzical look, "What the fuck?"

Abby rolls the rug into a ball and squeezes it against her chest, "In you go," she says while motioning to the door.

"Go where?"

"Quit it, okay. I think I feel a migraine coming on and I'm not in the mood because *someone* finished all the goddamn aspirin."

"Quit what?"

"Go sit down there for a bit. Clear out the crazy. I'm going upstairs to lay down. My headaches are starting to get bad and I think it might be serious."

Abby drops the rug on the floor and climbs the stairs while rubbing her temples. "Don't take forever though. I need you to mow the lawn, and fix the plumbing, and pay for the heat, and fix broken things, and get the mail, and..." she trails off as I watch her slippered feet step up out of my view.

"Abby?" I call.

No response.

What is she doing to me? Is she purposely keeping me in the dark? Is this some kind of fucked up psychological thing? Is she testing me? Is this what marriage is? Is she trying to decide if I'm worthy of fatherhood? If so, I can save her the trouble and tell her flat out, "I'M NOT!" But she genuinely seems to think that I

70

know what I can't possibly know. What would make her think that? What happened in those months of blacked-out time? How did I forget what is pretty much a lifetime of memories?

I turn my attention to the door in the floor.

And what's with this river business?

I stand and pull the metal handle on the door. A set of stairs lead to somewhere. Somewhere dark. I remove the 1216 badge Zippo from my pocket and illuminate the uncertainty. Once again, I'm stepping into the darkness led only by the light of my father's nicotine addiction.

The stairs go on for longer than I expected. If I was counting, which I wasn't, I'd say there were fifty, maybe even sixty creaky wooden steps. As I reach the bottom, I no longer need the Zippo as there appears to be some kind of light source down here. Something like natural moonlight, but considering I'm in a place beneath the secret room in the basement of my former father's former home, I can't imagine it is. I'll plan to investigate later, but I know I never will.

I look to the ground to realize that I'm standing in grass and about 25 feet in front of me is an honest to god river. In the grand scheme of all that's raging and white watery, I wouldn't call it the Mighty Mississippi, but regardless, it's still fucking weird.

It's laid out like a subway stop, if you can imagine the platform covered in nicely maintained grass while the track is filled with flowing water. The bank of the river is lined with green bushes growing purple flowers and blackish berries that bear a striking similarity to the ones Abby forced me to eat. I could still be in the midst of some kind of extended, or possibly permanent trip as a result of those fucking things. Which, now that I think of it, would be a fine explanation for there being a fucking river underneath my house. But that doesn't change the fact that I'm standing here with no hope of seeing this nonsense come to an end anytime soon.

As I walk closer to the water, I look left to see that the river extends into a tunnel. I look right to see the same thing, but on the bank, farther down, I see a man sitting in a lawn chair. I curiously walk toward him and notice that he's a chubby, balding man, and he's wearing a Hawaiian shirt. A fishing pole with its line in the water is jammed in the grass next to his chair. As I get closer, I can see that he's whittling a piece of a wood with a knife that I never thought I would see in real life. A hunting knife with the word PSYCHO etched into the blade. My hands slightly tremble as I approach the man. He looks up to me, and my trembling turns to full on shaking as I see a familiar face: mustache, sweaty brow, tuna in the corner of his mouth.

"You," I say.

The man smiles, wipes his right hand on his pants, and holds it for a shake, "Roy Beluga, pleased to meet ya again, Mr. Groff."

I take his hand and he nearly crushes my bones with his meaty mitt. "Have a seat, kiddo," he says with a nod to the grass next to his chair. I sit and feel the moisture from the grass soak into the seat of my pants. "Do you like fishing?" he asks with his eyes on the river.

"No," I say, "not at all."

"I love it myself," he says, "relaxing."

I nod and mutter, "Mm."

"Nothing's biting today though," he says. "Not yet, at least."

I watch the water gently flow past the fishing line. "I saw you jump into traffic," I finally say to the man. "I saw you die."

He smiles, "Yeah, it'll take a hell lot more than that to take out ol' Roy Beluga," he says.

I look up into those dead, bloodshot eyes.

"I guess It wasn't finished with me yet," he says with a shrug. "Guess I'm still necessary."

I pull my knees to my chest. "I don't understand."

Roy reaches into his shirt pocket and removes a cigar. He holds it me, "Got a light?"

I nod and hand him the Zippo. He torches the end of the stogy and drops the lighter into his pocket.

He puffs several times like a locomotive as it leaves the station."Thanks, pal," he says. "Say, would you do me another favor?"

"Maybe," I say.

He leans forward with stiff groan and reaches for his back pocket. As he does, I see a small revolver tucked into his belt. My face flushes and my head heats as I think he's going for the gun when he pulls a small, rolled, paperback book from his pocket. "Will you sign this for me?" he says and hands me a book. I unroll it to see a black cover that reads:

The Psycho Killer Down the Street
A bunch of stories that are connected
by
Daniel Groff

"Where did you get this?" I ask.

"Bought it."

"You bought it?"

He nods.

And I connect the dots for once. "Roy Beluga. BELUGA_WHALE_69. You're the guy, huh?"

"I'm the guy," he says.

I look at the book and smile. "This is pretty weird, Roy," I say.

Roy goes for that same shirt pocket, pulls a click pen, and hands it to me. "What can I say?" he says, "I'm a fan."

I open the book to the title page, hold the pen, think for a beat, and then quickly scribble:

ROY,
LIFE IS NOT THAT GREAT.
YOUR FRIEND (?),
DANIEL Groff

"Thanks," he says after I hand it back to him. "I'll treasure this shit forever." He rolls it up, sticks it into his pocket, and settles back into his seat.

We both stare at the river as he picks up the Psycho knife and returns to whittling. I look to the knife. "Where did you get that?" I ask.

He shrugs.

"You know it's from my book, right?"

He nods, "Yup."

"Did you make it?" I ask.

He shakes his head, "Nope."

"So you just have it?"

"Yup," he says.

I peek at the wood in his hand and can't figure out what he might be making. "What are you whittling?" I ask.

"Got no idea. It's probably a duck or some shit," he says.

I watch him carve into the wood.

"I'll probably find out when it's done," he says. "Then I'll probably know."

I stare at the blade as Roy sucks his smoke and chips away at the ambiguous block of nothing in his thick hands.

"Ya know, this is where we come from," Roy says, raising his eyes toward the river.

"Who's we?" I ask.

"We is us," he says. "All of us."

"Us as in… us?" I say patting my chest.

He nods.

"Abby?" I ask.

He nods.

"What is this river?" I ask. "Where did it come from?"

Roy shrugs.

"Someone must've made it."

He shrugs again. "I like to say It did it."

"It?"

"It," he says.

"Is It The Everything?"

Roy shrugs.

I watch the water run by and listen to the sound of Roy whittling his whatever.

"So this thing makes people?" I ask.

"Not makes. Delivers," he says.

"From where?"

"There."

"Where's there?"

"The place up above."

"Heaven?" I say.

Roy rests the blade against the wood and turns to me, "What are you six?"

"I don't know! I'm just asking," I say.

"Fuck that," he says. "Fuck that right now." He looks at me for another beat with absolute disappointment before he returns to whittling.

I don't know why my question was so bonkers, but it apparently was. I guess when you live in a world with magical rivers, suddenly pregnant wives, toxic berry trips, and formerly dead fat dudes with names as ludicrous as Roy Beluga, heaven is a pretty absurd concept.

I stare at the river and look back to him, "Roy, when you leapt in front of that car..."

But I'm cut off by the sound of Roy's fishing reel unspooling rapidly.

"Shit!" he yelps, drops the wood and grabs the pole from the ground while still clutching the knife. The pole bends and dips as Roy locks onto the reel's handle and tries to turn it away from the river.

"Fuck me! This one's got ahold of it!" he says, stands, and drops the cigar. He's now in a tug o' war with some kind of sub-basement river beast and he seems to be losing. Roy bites his mustache with his bottom teeth and sweat drips from his sizable (and already super sweaty) forehead. "I'll getcha, ya fuckin' bastard!" he shouts with all of his internal Ahab.

I jump to my feet and reach for the pole to help as Roy is yanked into the river, pole first. His hefty body splashes into the water like a kid doing a cannonball and he's taken by the river into the tunnel before I can process what I'm seeing.

"Roy!" I yell.

But there's nothing. Roy Beluga is gone. Gone to whatever place this river goes. I look to my feet and find the unfinished, unknowable wooden thing that Roy was carving and pick it up. I look back down the tunnel and thumb the notches made by the Psycho blade. "Where did you get that knife, Roy?" I say.

I turn away to see Abby and a little boy, both in swimsuits, dripping wet. They're picking berries from the bushes along the river.

Abby sees me and stands straight; her belly flat, her damp hair brown. She smiles and wipes her brow with a gloved hand that clutches a handful of green leaves. She looks down to the boy, pats him on the back, and whispers something in his ear. He runs toward me. His wet hair a mess of little boy hair and his face small and eager. He must be five years-old.

He stops at my feet and holds a balled fist to me. I open my palm and he drops a half-dozen berries into it. I look from the berries to the boy and smile.

"Eat the berries, Daddy," the boy says.

And for some reason, I eat the berries without complaint.

CHAPTER SEVENTEEN
Negative Noodle

Back in the Volvo out front of Abby's place, Lane poured through it all. Did that lady beat up herself? Is she some kind of freak? Is she nuts? She seemed so nice, he thought.

He looked at the house and took a breath and was struck by a pang of guilt. Why did he feel like he did something wrong? He didn't even understand why he was there in the first place. None of this was his fault. It was out of his hands. Wasn't it?

He turned his attention to the manila folder and peeled back its cover to find sheets of old, curled paper covered in writing that was scrawled in pencil. It was like a child wrote the pages. It was all laid out like a story, with a title on the first page:

"*The Psycho Killer Down the Street,*" Lane read aloud. "By Dan —"

"Mr. Laszlo?" A man's quivering voice interrupted.
Lane startled and spun and dropped his jaw when he laid eyes on the handle of the knife that was jammed into the top of the mustachioed man's balding head.
"My name is Roy Beluga and I was wondering if you would help me."
"Shit, man!" Lane shouted.
"I'm sorry. I didn't mean to frighten you."
"You got a knife in your head!" Lane said, now noticing that the man's hair and Hawaiian shirt were soaking wet.

"I know, Mr. Laszlo. But that's not important now."

"Oh no?"

"No, what's important is that I'm in your car, and I'm with you, and you're going to take me to your home."

"How did you get in my car?"

"It was unlocked. I opened the door and got into it. Now please take me to your home."

"Why would I do that?"

"Because you have to."

"You're fucking nuts! I'm taking you to a hospital."

Lane turned and cranked the ignition when the cock of a gun halted him. He turned again to see the barrel in his mug. Roy was so weak he could barely aim the piece.

"No hospitals, please. Take me back to your place."

"You're gonna bleed to death."

"Don't worry, all I need is some orange juice and I'll be fine. Trust me. Take me back to your place and it'll be good."

"I don't think that's such a good idea, pal."

Roy mustered up enough to press the wet steel against Lane's nose. "Mr. Laszlo...please...it's important."

With a heavy sigh, Lane gave up. He reluctantly turned to the wheel, shot the knife one more look in the rearview, and started the engine.

CHAPTER EIGHTEEN

The Psycho Killer Down the Street Part 6: A Prisoner in Hell

Daniel Groff Jr.
Grade 3
December 20, 1989

Hours after my defeat of the Psycho Killer Down the Street, I was wondering what was going to happen next. I started to walk but I watched the ground closely to make sure there were no holes leading to the flames of Hell below. Suddenly a huge hole opened up in front of me but I jumped back and yelled, "Ha! I got a little smarter didn't I, Satan?"

But then a hole opened up right where I was standing. BOOM! I hit the ground. Satan came out, "You are a good fighter, but now you must die!"

I grabbed a very sharp stone and stabbed Satan in the stomach. He picked me up and threw me against the wall. He sliced my face with his nails and stabbed me in the shoulder. He grabbed my throat and started choking me. I stabbed his hand and he let go. I climbed up onto his shoulders and jumped up out of the hole and Satan followed. He hit me in the face and threw me through a window and slammed me into a wall. I kicked him in the stomach and in the head ten times. I punched him in the face twice. I kicked him again. He grabbed me by the throat and said, "You suffer eternal fire!"

POOF! Suddenly we were in Hell again. His demons started flying all around me and I was in some kind of glass cube.

"Ahhhhhh! I'm a prisoner in the Flames of Hell!"

The end?

CHAPTER NINETEEN

Delivery

And Abby knocks on my door.

"Daniel?" she calls.
"What is it?" I say.
"Can you open this please?"
My workbench is barricading the door. I'm writing and I'm drinking and it's my room and it's my time and I don't want any visitors.
"What do you want?" I ask.
"It's important, Daniel. I need to tell you something."
I pause for a several seconds and think. I feel anxious. I feel strange. I feel annoyed.

"Now!" she yells.

I sigh, screw the cap on my bottle of Lonely Sparrow Whiskey, and jam it in a drawer. I leave my desk, push the workbench to the side, unlock the dead bolt, and open the door.

"WHAT!" I shout.

She hands me a large cardboard box, "This came for you."
"What is it?" I say, taking it from her.
She shrugs as I place the box on the floor. "You've been down here a long time," she says. "I feel like we never see you anymore."
"How long has it been?" I say and tear the tape from the top

of the box and pull open the flaps.

She pauses and clasps the top of her bathrobe. "You can't be serious," she says.

I shoot her a look that communicates exactly how serious I am.

"We haven't seen you for more than ten minutes at a time for like six months," she says. "I hope what you've been doing is worth it."

Lost more time. Wonderful. Fuck everything. "Nothing is worth nothing," I say while digging through the packing peanuts.

"What's that supposed to mean?" she says.

"It's not supposed to mean anyth—" I pause as my hand lands on something hard. Something cold. Something that feels like...

"Is that a fucking gun?" Abby says.

I pull it from the box, pointing it toward the ceiling. I look to her, confused.

"Did you order that?" she says.

"I don't think so."

"Then who did?"

I shake my head, look back to the box, and dig with my gun-free hand.

"I don't know what to say to this," she says. "You're slipping more and more and I think—"

From beneath the peanuts I pull a rectangular box that reads: Inkom Self-Defense .45 ACM 230 Grain Hollow Point Ammunition.

"Oh great," she says, "it came with bullets too."

I look back to the gun and tighten my grasp on the grip. It feels good. It feels real. It feels like something.

"I don't want that thing in my house," Abby says.

"I need to learn how to shoot it," I say.

"Did you hear me, Daniel?" she says.

"There's probably some videos online that I can watch," I say.

Abby puts her hands on her hips and bends toward me, "Did you hear me? I said, I don't want that thing in my house."

"I can set up a target in the backyard," I say while sliding my finger onto the trigger.

"Listen to me, Danny. I said, I don't want a gun in my house! Especially not with—"

"It's not your fucking house, Abby."

She drops her arms and frowns. "What?"

"Now go upstairs." I say.

"How could you talk to me like that?"

"Go. The fuck. Upstairs." I say and slide my eyes from the gun to her. "Now."

CHAPTER TWENTY

Juice

Roy plopped on Lane's couch and Lane sat on a chair across from him. Roy rested the gun on his damp thigh and kept it pointed toward Lane.

"When you donate blood they give you orange juice and cookies," Roy said after he sucked down some Tropicana, "do you have any cookies?"

"No, sorry, Roy."

"I would love a fucking cookie." Roy said.

"I'm sorry, pal."

"Maybe in a few minutes we can go get some?"

"Sure."

"In a few minutes though, okay?"

"Okay."

Roy rested his head against the back of the couch, soaking the spot. He looked at the ceiling and sighed, "I can't help but feel like this is gonna turn out for the best," he said.

Lane laughed.

Roy raised his head and smiled.

"Did you do that to yourself, Roy?"

"Yes," He said and laid his head back. "Well, kind of. It was more like an accident. But everything's gonna be okay."

"I bet," Lane said and drank from his juice. He realized that it was pulp-free and immediately felt the aggravation because he intended to buy the super-duper pulpy kind, but must've grabbed the wrong carton from the shelf in the supermarket. "Goddammit," he said under his breath.

"What's the matter, Mr. Laszlo?"

"Nothing, don't worry about it."

"Okay. No worries. No worries. No worries." Roy said like a rapid-fire mantra.

"Cool, Roy," Lane said with pause. He took another sip. "So what do you want from me?" he said after the swallow.

"I don't know."

"Oh, good."

"I'm just so fucking happy!"

"You sure about that?"

"It's weird though… I mean…" Roy smiled, "This place feels different. Like I feel happy. But it's forced. Like I have to be good and feel good. Like, it's great. Everything is great."

Lane squinted and analyzed. "I suppose," he said.

"Everything's okay."

"I know, Roy. You already said that."

"It's the accidental Dutchness that gets me."

"What's that?"

"Accidental Dutchness, Mr. Laszlo. It's strange."

Lane stared into his beverage for a beat. "What's that mean?"

"I've been accidentally speaking Dutch."

"Hm."

Roy giggled, "Fucked up, right?"

"C o u l d   y o u   s p e a k   D u t c h   r i g h t   n o w ?"

"No, it happens every once in a while. Like I said, *accidental* Dutchness."

"That's odd," Lane said.

"They say the Dutch are a happy people," Roy said.

"Who says that?"

Roy paused and thought for a beat. "Who the fuck knows?" he laughed.

"Is that why there's a knife in your head? Because of the Dutch?"

"No."

"Then why is it there?"

Roy lifted his head and allowed his weight to fall forward so his elbows rested on his knees, wavering like an shithouse in a hurricane.

"You familiar with the concept of optimism, Mr. Laszlo?"

"Of course."

"Sometimes optimism gets so…" Roy smiled like puppeteers were tugging the corners of his mouth with invisible strings from the ceiling. "…positively…" Roy's words seemed blocked, he tried to continue but his face turned a shade of yellow, and he seemed as if he could…

"BARRRFFFFF!"

Lane jumped to his feet. "Oh, Roy! What the fuck?"

"I'm sorry, Mr. Laszlo!"

"C'mon, Roy! You puked all over my floor!"

"Niets is goed!" Roy said breathlessly.

"What?"

"Everything's gonna be okay!" Roy said while staring into the puddle of vomit between his Velcro sneakers.

"What's going on here? Tell me right now!"

"I don't know. It's strange. Different. Not real. I don't think I can… I mean… I know… I know I can… I just…"

"Roy?"

"This is why there's a knife in my noodle, Mr. Laszlo."

"Because of puking?"

"Because I feel so fucking good! I'm smiling and good and people want to love me. People want me to love them. I want to love and be loved and love love."

And there was a pause.

An awkward as hell pause.

"Well, shit, man." Lane said and drained the last of his juice. "Refill?" he motioned his empty glass to Roy.

Roy placed the gun on the couch and poured the remaining juice down his throat. He tapped the bottom of glass ensuring that every drop dripped down the gullet. He pulled the glass away, burped, wiped his mouth with his wrist, and held the glass to Lane, "If it's not too much trouble. I could use a rinse, ya know? I think the OJ is working."

Lane followed the trail of blood and water that ran from Roy's head to the faded upholstery on dead Aunt Nina's couch to the puddle of puke on the floor. Aunt Nina died while praying right where that puddle was left by Roy Beluga, the balding, middle-aged, slightly overweight, Hawaiian shirt-wearing weirdo with a knife in his skull. As Lane stared into the redness and vomit he thought about Abby's bloody nose, and the screaming, and the crying.

He sighed, walked into the kitchen, and opened the fridge. "So what brought you to my backseat, Roy?" he asked as he took the cardboard carton from the top shelf. It stood next to a package of tofu that Lane was planning to make for dinner. He had found a new stir-fry recipe online and he was dying to try it. But now, since Roy was bleeding in his living room, he didn't think he'd have time.

"Well, I figured you could help me," Roy said.

"How?"

"I have these papers…" Roy leaned up and pulled a folded, waterlogged, paper-clipped stack of pages, and a small black paperback book from his back pocket.

"Where did you get them?"

"There's always paper everywhere," Roy said as he stuck the black book back into his pocket.

Lane walked to Roy and took the pages. "I suppose that's true. What's that black book?"

"It's nothing," Roy said.

"You've got some pretty roomy pockets, Roy."

Roy chuckled, "Please look at the thing in your hand," he said.

Lane read the first page. It was titled, *Lane Laszlo and the Broken Everything*.

"What the fuck?" Lane said and continued reading:

Eggs. Black coffee. Half a grapefruit. He popped the toast before it was done because he was sick of waiting. He was already waiting. Why wait for more, he thought. He buttered the half-toasted bread and plopped in the old recliner and flipped on the tube. *The Good, the Bad and the Ugly* was on. He smiled and settled in.

Lane looked to Roy. "You don't know where this came from?" he asked.

"No."

"Did someone give them to you?"

"No, I don't think so."

"So they showed up in your pocket?"

"Yes, and it's weird. There's this shit, this shit that I know and this shit that I understand, and I got this need and pull and drive to tell it to you."

"What do you mean?"

"I know that you need information and I know that I got information. That's it."

"So let me get this straight, you found these crazy ass pages that feature some kind of story about me, you don't know how they got there, you don't know who could've put them there, and you don't know why they're there. But you decided to track me down, get in the backseat of my car, and wait for me, with a gun, while dripping wet and slowly bleeding to death from the knife wound in the top of your head."

"Yes."

Lane pointed at the camera in the corner, its red light blinking in that same obnoxious way it always blinked. "Do you expect me to believe that you're not involved with the assholes who watch me and call me and give me these weird fucking things to do all the time? You expect me to believe all this shit is random?"

"I don't expect you to believe anything, Mr. Laszlo. I expect you to help me."

"What is it that you think I can do for you, Roy?"

"I think you can find the person who did this to me," he said, pointing at the knife in his skull.

"I thought you did that to you."

"No, before that, the guy who did this to all of us."

"And who's that?"

"Daniel Groff."

"Daniel Groff?"

"Daniel Groff did it all."

"That name sounds familiar."

"He's a person. He's a guy. He's a thing."

"What did he do?"

"He did his pain. He did his loneliness. He did his misery."

"His misery put a knife in your head?"

"His misery basically put knives in all of our heads."

Lane tightened his lips, "So what do you want me to do?"

"I want you to find him."

"And then what?"

"Kill him."

Lane leapt to his feet. "Great! So now you want me to fucking kill people?" He turned to the camera. "You guys are pushing it this time! You fucking pricks are doing some shit, aren't you?" he shouted and hurled his empty juice glass at the camera, shattering it against the wall, nearly missing the device.

"Calm down, Mr. Laszlo." Roy said.

Lane screamed, "This is stupid! This is stupid and unnecessarily cryptic and dumb and I hate it!"

"So do I, Mr. Laszlo," Roy said.

"So then let's stop, Roy. Let's stop being dumb."

Roy leaned forward and rested his elbows on his knees again. "But then what would we be?" he said.

"What's that supposed to mean?" Lane said.

"If we're not dumb, we can't learn, right?"

"I suppose."

"Then we won't grow. We won't change. We won't be the best us we can be. Right?"

Lane frustratingly exhaled, and sat next to Roy, "What do you want from me, man? For real."

"You're a private eye, Mr. Laszlo. Help me. Investigate. And then fix it. Fix the Everything."

"What's the Everything?"

"You're a private eye!"

Lane took a deep breath and crossed his arms and leaned back against the couch. "I hate to break your heart, pal, but I'm not a private eye."

"Yes, you are."

"No, I'm not."

"But it's in these pages."

Lane shook his head, "Don't matter."

"Then what are you?"

"I don't know," he said with a shrug, "but I'm not that."

"Well, then how am I supposed to fix the Everything?" Roy said.

"What do you want me to do? What do you want me to say?"

"Daniel Groff is breaking the Everything. The cycle keeps

going. He put things in our heads. Misery things. Angry things. And now bullshit, optimistic, happy things."

"Do you realize what you're saying?" Lane said.

"Yes!"

"You're an idiot, man."

"I know. And it's okay, Mr. Laszlo."

"You're an idiot and you're getting on my nerves."

"Mr. Laszlo..."

Lane stood. "Fuck you, Roy! You show up in my car, put a gun in my face, force me to take you to my house, you bleed on my couch, you drink my juice, you puke on my floor, you fuck up my dinner plans. You've pissed me off, Roy. You've pissed me off and now I'm saying fuck you! Okay? Fuck you right in your fucking knife wound."

Roy grabbed the gun from the couch and pointed it at Lane. "I'm gonna kill you, Mr. Laszlo."

"No, you're not."

"Yes, I am. I'm gonna kill you."

"Roy, shut up. Shut the fuck up!"

"No, you shut up, Mr. Laszlo. You shut up!"

"Put the gun down, Roy."

"No."

"Put it down!"

"No!"

"If you don't put that gun down, I'm gonna—"

Roy pulled the hammer and angled the gun at Lane's head. "Tref te sterven voorbereidingen, Mr. Laszlo."

"What?"

"I. Don't. Know."

"You Dutch speaking fuck!" Lane said and leapt at Roy, tackling him against the back of the couch. They wrestled for the gun and rolled onto the floor. Roy forced the gun into Lane's face, slid his finger onto the trigger, and started to squeeze when Lane grabbed the handle of the knife and yanked it from Roy's head.

"Oh my God!" Roy screamed as blood spouted like a bidet in a fancy hotel room.

Lane watched Roy's eyes roll back. The life drained from his face in disgusted horror as the blood flowed into a pool on the floor. "Oh fuck, Roy. Don't die in my house!"

Roy slowly sank into the pool like a hot bath.

"Roy!" Lane shouted. "I'm calling an ambulance."

Lane moved for the phone when Roy locked his hand around his arm, halting him. "Mr. Laszlo, no…"

"I can't have you die right now, Roy. It's not a good thing."

Roy raised a lifeless finger and pointed to the knife still clutched in Lane's fist.

Lane turned and noticed the blade had the word PSYCHO etched into it and at its pointed tip, a round, bloody blob, like an undercooked boiled egg, was dangling.

"The happiness…" Roy whispered.

Lane looked from Roy to the blob and back to Roy, "What?"

"The misery, Mr. Laszlo… The misery and happiness… it's gone."

"I should call an ambulance."

"No, Mr. Laszlo… the peace… the peace is… fine."

"Roy, what the fuck are you—"

Roy released Lane's arm, and wilted away, splashing into the puddle of blood. Lane looked to him and watched as Roy smiled, closed his eyes, and died.

"Roy?" Lane shouted. "Roy?"

Silence.

"Fuck!"

Lane paused a few beats and stared into Roy's extremely dead face. He turned to the goopy globule on the end of the knife and got to his feet. He carried it into the kitchen, holding his hand beneath the thing, careful not to drop it. He took a clear plastic bag from a cupboard and shook the globule from the blade into it. He held the bag to the fluorescent light in the ceiling and examined the slimy grossness.

It was translucent and Lane noticed some kind of shape inside. He gently slid the globule out of the bag onto the counter and carefully sliced into it with the Roy's PSYCHO head knife. It popped like a blister and a squirt of creamy juice shot Lane in the face. "Oh, fu—" he began, but paused as he stared at the small wooden duck that had emerged from within the hunk of mush.

Lane squinted, grimaced, pinched the duck, and held it to the light.

"Daniel Groff," he said, "I don't like the sound of that."

CHAPTER TWENTY-ONE

The Psycho Killer Down the Street Part 7:
Possessed

Daniel Groff Jr.
Grade 3
January 3, 1990

Satan magically walked through the wall of my glass cube. He smacked me in the face and threw me against a wall. He punched me three times. He smashed a rock on my head. I was bleeding bad. I got up and kicked him in the stomach and kicked him in the nuts. He grabbed me by my throat and looked into my eyes closely. He said, "Do you know why you are here?"

"To kill you, Satan!"

"No, you are here because you are my son!"

"No way!" I screamed.

Suddenly, I started shaking. I broke out in a sweat. My eyes turned yellow. My pupils turned beet red. I grew blood red fangs. I grew black three-inch nails. I started bulging out with muscles and my clothes ripped off. I grew two huge wings out of my back. THUMP! Satan's body fell. His soul was possessed inside me!

I roared like a lion. I threw up all over. My wings started flapping. I flew around all over and I smashed my head against a wall.

Am I really the devil?

The end?

CHAPTER TWENTY-TWO
Stuffed Idiot

In the backyard, I hang that stupid one-eyed doll that my father had sitting on his workbench from a tree. It dangles from its arm and slowly spins as I take a drink, clutch my new handgun, close an eye, and aim it at the stuffed idiot's head.

The video from the Internet told me to squeeze the trigger. Don't pull it. Squeeze it.

And so I do.

And so I miss.

"You didn't get him, Daddy," I hear a voice say from behind me. I turn to look and see the kid with his hands in his pockets rocking back and forth from his heels to his toes.
"No, I didn't," I say.
"You probably gotta aim better," he says.
"You're probably right, kiddo," I say and swig the last of the Lonely Sparrow and drop the empty bottle onto the dead grass. "C'mon over here."
He sprints to me, I snatch him up, and hold him with my left arm as we face the stuffed boy. "Wanna help?" I say.
He nods.
I raise the gun, pointing the muzzle skyward. "Put your hand on my hand," I say. He does, resting his small right hand on mine.
"Let's see if we can't get this guy this time," I say.

"Yeah!" he says with a smile.

He slides his finger over mine as I place it onto the trigger. I straighten my arm as far as possible, making sure he can still reach the gun.

"Now look down the barrel," I say. He closes his right eye and leans his head in front of mine, peering along the top of the gun. "Are we on target?" I say.

He reaches out with his left hand and raises our arms about an inch. "Now we are."

I watch the stuffed boy. He spins on, clueless about what he's going to experience, and I close my right eye. "Now, you gotta squeeze the trigger, kiddo," I say. "Don't pull it. Squuuuueeeeeeeeeeze it."

And so we do.

And we get him.

Stuffing from the doll scatters into the air as the bullet nearly tears it in two.

"Got him!" we scream in unison, laughing.

"What did I say?" Abby says from the sliding glass back door. She watches us, arms folded.

I turn to her as my smile dissipates and I lower the gun.

"What did I say, Daniel?" she says again.

"We're just having some fucking fun," I say.

Abby eyes the empty bottle at my feet and shakes her head. She reaches her arms out and looks to the kid. "Come here, kiddo," she says.

He wiggles free from me, drops to the ground, and runs to her. She picks him up. "Are you okay?" she asks him.

He doesn't answer.

"I don't want you going near Daddy when he has that gun," she says, "it's dangerous."

The boy looks down in shame. "I'm sorry," he says as tears well in his eyes.

"You didn't do anything wrong, kiddo," I say. "Your mother's being an uptight bitch is all. We were having fun."

"You're drunk," she says.

"Oh please," I say.

Abby pulls the boy tighter against her chest and locks eyes with me. "I don't even know you anymore," she says.

I shrug and slightly stumble. "When did you even know me at all?" I say.

She shakes her head and looks to the gun. "I don't want that thing near my son."

I look down to it and thumb the hammer.

"I mean it," she says.

I meet her eyes. "You can't fucking tell me what to do," I say. "I'm in control of this shit."

She tightens her lips and sighs. "Finish the fucking book, Daniel. Please," she says and turns, sliding the glass door closed behind her.

I watch her walk away through the glass. I lift the gun, pointing it at the back of her head. I see the kid as he watches me over her shoulder.

And the gun goes off.

CHAPTER TWENTY-THREE

Lonely Sparrows

Lane sat on the floor next to the fat man's body and flipped through the pages. He scanned the prose, the random notes, the sloppiness. "No making heads or tails of this mess," he said.

He turned to a random page and found this:

1. GIVE DEPTH TO THE DILEMMA.

2. WHICH IS THE EVERYTHING?

3. EVERY SOUL IS A FRAGMENT OF A FRAGMENT OF A FRAGMENT

4. LONELY SPARROWS!

5. THE CONFABULATIONS OF...

6. THE EVERYTHING IS IT

7. WHAT IS THIS FUCKING MECHANISM OF DEATH?

8. PEOPLE WHO TAP INTO THIS "BOX" BECOME CARRIERS FOR "LOST" SOULS.

9. FACILITATION OF THE COMING OF THE EVERYTHING-EVERYTHING.

10. IS THE BERRY?

11. DANIEL

12. GROFF

13. BLIGHTED DANIELS

14. BLIGHTED BRAINS

15. ATROPINE IS GOOD

16. WHAT (WHY) DID HE (WE) DO (THAT) TO ABBY (MIA)?

And Lane paused, squinting at the name Abby. What *did* he do to Abby? And who was Mia?

One mysterious lady name at a time, he thought. He needed to talk to Abby again. But how? When he last saw her she accused him of things he couldn't have possibly done. There was no way she'd speak with him, not after threatening to call the cops. If Lane went back to her place and she freaked out again, he'd end up in more of a mess than he was already in, especially with a Hawaiian shirt-wearing stiff on his carpet.

And speaking of the stiff, Lane looked into Roy's lifeless eyes and said, "Sorry, I had to do what I did, Roy."
Roy responded by still being dead.
"What do you think I should do now?"
Still dead.
"You think I should go back and talk to that lady?"
Still dead.
"I know, I know, she might lose it again and I could be fucked."
"But you could be even more fucked if you don't get to the bottom of this mess, Mr. Laszlo," Roy said. Kidding. He was still dead.
"That's true, Roy. That's a good point. If I don't talk to her

about all this nuttiness, I might never figure out whatever the fuck this is. And then where would I be? I'd probably be even more fucked, wouldn't I?"

Still dead.

"Okay. You're right. I'm doing it. I'll sweet talk her and iron things out and get some info. I can do this, Roy. I know I can."

Still dead.

"Thanks, Roy. You're a chum. Sorry again for doing that thing to you. You seemed like you might be an okay fella, if it wasn't for the knife in your head, and the gun, and the irrational behavior and whatnot."

Lane covered his body with a blanket and remembered the manila envelope that Abby handed him before the chaos got chaotic.

He opened it, looked at the first page of child-like scrawls again, and read the title at the top of the white-lined paper that was clearly ripped from one of those black and white composition notebooks, "The Psycho Killer Down the Street," he said, "cheesy as shit."

He flipped through page after page of penciled words. It appeared to be a series of short stories; each one building upon the next; each one about some kid who was doing endless battle with a scarred lunatic with a knife; each one worse than the last.

"This is fucking junk," he said. "How could this have to do with anything? And why the fuck does this 'mystery' involve so much dumb writing?"

He looked to Roy for assistance but not surprisingly, Roy remained dead.

"I don't know either, man," Lane said and searched Roy's pockets. He found nothing but a Zippo lighter adorned with a silver police badge reading the number 1216, a slim black paperback book of that dumb ass thing called *The Psycho Killer Down the Street*, and a click pen. He got to his feet and looked to Roy Beluga, deceased head-stabber and Hawaiian shirt enthusiast, and dropped the book, pen, pages, lighter, and knife into a messenger bag. He slung it over his shoulder and said, "Let's go talk to Abby. Again."

CHAPTER TWENTY-FOUR

The Psycho Killer Down the Street Part 8: Satan Ate My Soul

Daniel Groff Jr.
Grade 3
January 17, 1990

My eyes opened slowly. I looked around. I was in a red room. There was fire everywhere but it was dark. I looked up and saw a little bit of light coming in through a hole in the ceiling. So I started to climb and climb and climb and climb until I got to the light. I reached my hand through the hole and pulled myself up and out.

I felt something sharp on my back as I climbed out of the hole and turned to see Satan's eyes staring at me. I was climbing out of his mouth!

He breathed deep and spit me out against a wall. I hit my head.

He said, "I don't know what to do. I want to help you, but you won't let me. I love you, kiddo. Don't you understand?" And he hit me.

I punched him in the face. He pushed me away and punched me in the face and smashed my head against a wall. He kicked me in the face. I hit him with a rock. I punched him in the stomach. He slammed my head against a rock six times. He charged me with his horns. I moved out of the way and his horns got stuck in the wall. I got a big sharp rock and stabbed it through his back. He passed out. I thought he might be dead but he wasn't. I sat down to think for a second.

Suddenly, I saw the worst sight ever.

The end?

CHAPTER TWENTY-FIVE

It's Happening Again

I don't know what I did. I don't know why I did what I did. I don't know why I am who I am.

I don't know if the real is here anymore. I don't know if the present is now anymore. I don't know if the future is coming anymore. I don't know what I don't know.

I think I'm plagiarizing his life.

I think he was plagiarizing my life.

I think It's plagiarizing our lives.

I think it's all happening at the same time.

I think It knows too much about us.

I think It's going to kill us.

So what's left to do? What's left to be? What's left of us?

Things are slipping. Things are changing.

Years are moving. Years are going.

I am changing. I am slipping.

I am nothing but words. Words are nothing but words.

None of this means anything.

But I feel guilt. I feel shame. I feel anger. I feel wrong. I don't think I'm in control of this anymore. I don't think it's me who is doing any of it. I think It's in charge and I think It wants more from us.

When the bullet shattered the glass she fell to the ground and screamed a scream that will never not echo in my mind. And my heart broke. It was wrong what I did. It was an accident what I did. It was on purpose what I did. It was me who did what I did. It was him who did what I did. It was It who did what I did. It was all of us.

And I ran through the back door, stepping over broken glass, and reached her just as she climbed to her feet, still clutching the screaming boy in her arms. Before I could speak, she was sprinting through the house and out the front door and into the car and gone down the street.

I could see that she was fine. The bullet missed. The bullet missed both of them. But she was gone. He was gone. I don't know if they'll ever come back.

And now I'm here. Typing. I'm typing these words. The words you are reading right now. I am typing these words and drinking this drink and I'm waiting. Waiting for something. Waiting for something real.

CHAPTER TWENTY-SIX

Hang In There

Lane knocked on the perfect door at 7 Milberg Place once again and noticed a smear of blood on the back of his hand. "Christ!" he said as he licked his thumb and went to work on it. What would this poor lady think if the guy she somehow believed slugged her showed up with blood on his hand? Wouldn't go over too well, Lane thought.

And she opened the door. Again.

"LANE!" she said a bit too happily. She held a pair of gardening shears in one gloved-hand and a bundle of those same green leaves with blackish berries in the other. "I was hoping you'd stop by."

"Wait…" Lane said. "This is…"

She set the shears onto a table next to the door, pulled a glove off her right hand, and went for the shake. "I'm Abby."

Lane apprehensively took her hand.

"I'm part of this whole thing," she said with that warm smile. "Are you okay, Abby?"
She smiled again. "Come on inside. I just made coffee."

Lane stepped through the door and immediately felt awful. The house was still good. It was still right. It still felt like a home.

But why was Abby acting like that whole thing didn't happen earlier? Why did it seem like she was playing the scene out exactly as it was before? What was the game here?

"How do you take it?" Abby asked on her way into the kitchen.

"Uh, black…" Lane said as if he was trying to remember his lines in a school play. He checked out the framed photos hanging on the walls once again. Still that same desperate looking kid at the zoo, in a park, in a backyard. And there were still those shots of a much younger, punky-looking Abby and a man with shaggy hair, a mustache, and a beat-up suit. But this time, he noticed one he hadn't seen before. It was of that shaggy-haired man looking way less shaggy and wearing a police uniform, proudly posed in front of the American flag.

Abby returned and handed Lane that same mug that showed a dead cartoon cat with a noose. "Hang in there, kiddo!" it still shouted.

"Piping hot cuppa black," she said with that same warmth as before.
"Thanks," Lane said. He was getting his lines right this time.
And Abby glanced at that photo of the shaggy man and she cooled again, "Want to sit down, Lane?"
And Lane followed her into the living room.

Lane figured the best way to figure out this business was to play along. Try to recreate the experience exactly as it was before. He'd have to see this through. Moment for moment. Word for word.

"So, as I said earlier, I was hoping you'd stop by." Abby said.
"Why is that?"
"Sit," she said motioning to the puffy white sofa.
Lane sat.
"I don't know," she said and sat on the love seat adjacent to the sofa. "Sometimes I think about you and I say, 'boy, I hope Lane stops by.'"

Lane stared uncomfortably.

Abby smiled, "You almost never do."

"Almost?"

"Well," she took a sip from her coffee, "you're here now."

Lane tried to force a friendly giggle, "So what does, you're involved in this whole thing, mean exactly?"

Abby shrugged, "I don't know. I mean, I know, but I don't know."

"Sounds strange," Lane said.

They both laughed.

"Yeah, I guess it's all pretty peculiar."

"Do you know what I do, Abby?"

"You're a private eye."

"Yeah... that's right," Lane said.

Abby shrugged and they stared. Lane couldn't remember what he was supposed to do now, but Abby continued, "Sometimes I think about where we are. Where we're going. Where we'll be. Where we came from." She shifted her gaze to Lane. "Sometimes I think about what put us here. What made us. All of the choices and randomness and messiness and meaninglessness. All of it. Sometimes I think about those things, and those things lead me to you." She leaned forward, "You're something to me, Lane. You're floating in my river with me. You're here, and I'm not alone." She reached out and touched his knee with her fingertips. "You're what I know," she said, "and that's good."

"But, for real this time, what does that mean?" Lane said.

Abby pulled back, "It doesn't matter."

"What doesn't?"

"It."

"What is IT?"

Abby shrugged.

Lane placed his mug on a coaster on the end table next to the couch and tried to get his lines correct. "Do you have *something* for me to investigate? A cheating husband thing? A missing business partner? Anything?"

Abby frowned. Lane continued to feel guilty. "Would that make it easier for you?"

"Yes," he said and meant it more than he meant it before. Lane was dealing with layers upon layers now, and he was getting frustrated.

Abby sighed and stood and walked into the other room.

Lane stewed further in his discomfort. He couldn't make heads or nothing out of this scene. Why was it replaying? Why was Abby playing along? Was he stuck in some kind of sci-fi bullshit thing? Did he hit his head? Did he crash his car? Was he laying in some hospital bed and this was his brain's last gasp before his mother (who he hadn't called in months) yanks the power cord, sending Lane tumbling into the afterlife? Was he already dead?

But Abby came back, right on cue. And she was a holding that manila folder. And her nose was bleeding, once again.

"I hope this helps you, Lane," she said with it extended to him.

As Lane took it, he pointed to her face.

She reached up and touched it. As she examined the blood, she shot Lane that horrible look of misery and confusion, "Why did you do this me?"

"I didn't do it." Lane said assertively, trying to alter the course of this dreadful afternoon any way he could.

"I thought this was over. I thought you said—" she cried and flung the folder, storming into the other room.

Lane stood. "Abby, we need to talk about th—"

She came back with the suitcase, "Take your shit and get the fuck out of here, you animal!"

Lane noticed that that badly bruised cheek had joined the blood dripping from her nostrils. "I didn't do that to you!"

"I don't know what I do to deserve this! I don't know why you have to make me suffer like this! What did I do? Aren't I good? Don't I treat you right?"

"This isn't—"

"Get the fuck out of here!" she screamed and flung the suitcase at him, this time smashing Lane in the nose, immediately crushing it flat and sending blood and snot streaming like the insides of a New Year's popper.

Lane shoved his fingers into his nostrils as if he was trying to stuff the blood back into his head, "Abby, please, I'm sorry!"

"Save your fucking sorries, you nasty piece of shit! I'm sick of this!" And she grabbed a steaming mug of coffee from the table next to the sofa and flung it into Lane's face, shattering it like a caffeinated grenade.

"AAAARRRGGGHH!" he screamed as the hot ceramic shards tore his skin.

"Now get the fuck out of here before I call the police AGAIN!" she screeched with even more than she had inside herself previously.

Through a haze of blood, pain, and coffee, Lane ran for the door.

Part Three

CHAPTER TWENTY-SEVEN

It's Berries

If I knew what I was doing, I'd do it. But I'm just here and I'm typing and I'm being. This is what I'm doing.

Abby. Words. Me. Some kid. Some house. Some life.
A chair. A desk. A typewriter. Some booze. Some berries. Some shit.

This is what I am. This is what I'm always going to be. Me. Me is me and there's no changing that. And the realization of that fucking sucks. I can sit here and be this and I can do this and I want that. But it is what it is and it's not what it's not. And that's it. That's it. That's it. That's it.

This kid is on the floor and he's playing with some toy while a woman is upstairs and she's doing what she's doing.

After I did the gun thing they came back and I cried and she cried and she forgave me and we moved on. And now time has moved on. I don't know how much time has moved on, but time has moved on.

And I'm here. And I'm me. I'm always me.

The want is the problem. The need is the problem. The something else is always something else. It will never be done. It will never stop. It will never be what it should be. Should. Should be. Should be doesn't exist. Is. Is is all there is.

And so I'll type. And I'll think. And I'll type. And I'll drink. And I'll die.

And that is it.
Because that is It.
And that is all.

I turn from the typewriter and look to the boy on the floor. "Hey, kiddo," I say. He looks from his truck to me.

"Run upstairs and get your old man another bottle, will ya?" I say while shaking the empty Lonely Sparrow Whiskey.

I've been letting him sit in here while I work. It's the least I can do. It's called quality time. It's called fatherly time.

He bites his tongue and pushes himself into a stand and sprints up the basement stairs.

I watch him until he's out of sight and I return to my machine and look at the black letters on the white page. Letters. Pages. Eyes. Readers. What the fuck is this shit? What the fuck am I doing? Do I honestly believe that someone will read this? Do I honestly believe someone will care?

A bowl of berries sits next to the typewriter and I grab a handful and throw them back and chew and swallow. As time goes on, I've built up a tolerance and it doesn't hit the way it used to. I need more. More. Always needing more. Always wanting more. Always more when it comes to need. Always need when it comes to want.

"What the fuck is this shit?" I say.

"What the fuck is this Everything?" I say.

And so I type.

CHAPTER TWENTY-EIGHT
A Fucking Scar

Lane wrapped a towel around a pile of ice cubes and pressed it to his bleeding, blistering face. "This is gonna leave a fucking scar," he said as he dropped onto the couch and peeled open the folder to find dozens of typed pages. He glanced to the security camera in the corner and stared at the orange juice pulp that had dried to the wall behind it. It resembled a citrus constellation and this thought struck Lane as funny in light of the face-full of mug Abby sent his way. Things may have gotten shitty for Lane Laszlo, but at least he still had his sense of humor.

He turned his attention to Roy's bodys on the floor and sighed, "How in the fuck did we get here, Roy?"

He looked back to the pages from Abby's folder and began to read what you're about to read.

Here we go.

1.

When Lane Laszlo was nine years-old, he lived in a world of pills and anger. He went his whole childhood without any friends. He chose to be alone. He chose to be quiet. He chose to wear old suits, like a miniature businessman. He chose to ramble, to drift, to wander. He liked to be outside. He liked to have a destination of uncertainty. He liked to be under the sky and in the sun. He liked to see the trees and the world. Every smell appealed to him, even the bad ones. He liked the smell of garbage trucks when they drove by and he liked the smell of skunk spray and he liked the smell of bus exhaust. Smells set his thoughts into motion. They made him realize that there was a life outside of his bedroom. There was a life outside of the screaming and the fighting. There was a life that he could be part of and when he was roaming and rambling and sniffing and seeing, he was part of it. He was happy to be free and free to be happy.

He called his bedroom The Cube of Doom. It was tiny and humid and depressing and infested with nasty, many-legged silverfish. They would crawl on the walls and sometimes they would walk on his face while he lay in bed. He once had a can of soda in his room and took a drink from it and got a mouthful of silverfish. It was torture for Lane. "The Cube" was like a jail-cell and if he wasn't outside, he was trapped in there, forced to listen to the pandemonium that would break out in the other rooms of the house.

The pandemonium came from his mom and dad. They hated each other. They hated being together but for some reason, they stayed together all the time. They were married for over twenty years and for the all the years that he could remember, they would spend their time screaming and fighting. They threw things. They broke things. They cursed a lot. They hated a lot. But they loved pills. Dad took them because they made him walk funny. They made him walk into walls and made his eyes glassy and made him laugh at nothing. Mom took them because she thought that they could cure her "sickness." Doctors told Mom that the "sickness" didn't exist but she didn't care. She didn't believe them. She knew it was there. Mom was sick, but not in the way that she thought. Mom was a different kind of sick.

Dad also loved his guns. His favorite was a handgun that he named Psycho.

Lane shopped at thrift stores because he could get suits for super cheap. One day, next to a box of ties, he found a little stuffed boy. It was missing an eye and had an oversized head and he looked sad and dirty and lonely and sick. Lane thought he was perfect. When he checked the price tag he was thrilled to discover that he was only seventy-five cents. He reached into his pocket to fish out the three quarters that he had left over from that week's lunch money. He bought the little fella and headed for home.

He set the boy on his bed and sat cross-legged with his chin perched on his inter-laced fingers and stared into the boy's lone eye. "What am I gonna call you?" he said to him.

He furrowed and squinted and looked hard into the black plastic eyeball. He was about to say the first name that popped into his brain when he heard Dad's voice from the other room.

"Lane!"

He paused, closed his eyes, and sighed. He could tell from the sound of Dad's voice that the weirdness was about to hit.

He grabbed the still nameless stuffed boy, walked into Dad's bedroom, and saw him sitting on the edge of his bed. He was glassy-eyed and red-faced and seemed like his brain was transmitting from another dimension. He waved Lane over and patted his leg, "Saddle up, kiddo."

As Lane approached, Dad grabbed him and propped him on his knee. He stroked his dirty blond hair and told him gently, "I need to tell you something, Lane. Something very, very important."

"Okay." Lane replied squeezing the stuffed boy tightly around the neck.
"Something's got me. I don't know what it is, but it's bad."
"What do you mean?" Lane asked.
"This thing is gonna kill me. It's gonna kill my head. Do you know about that?"
Lane wasn't sure what the correct answer was, "I don't know..."

"You bet you know!" Dad said. "I know you know! Just like HER!"

"What do you mean, Dad?"

He turned away as if something across the room distracted him. He stared in the direction of the imaginary sound for several seconds, and whispered, "Something's watching me, Lane. They're watching me. The ones in charge are spying on me." He turned back. His eyes opened wide like he only then noticed Lane was sitting on his knee. He wrapped his arms around him and squeezed the child, "I love ya, kiddo. I hope you know that."

Lane was frightened. "I know," he said.

Dad reached under his pillow and pulled out his handgun, the one he called Psycho. He pointed it toward the ceiling like he was preparing for a duel. He closed his eyes, took a deep breath, and tried to place the gun in Lane's right hand. Lane squeezed the stuffed boy tighter. Dad grunted, tugged the doll from his grasp, and tossed it across the room.

"Take it!" he said motioning the gun toward Lane.

Lane's trembling digits gripped the handle and pointed the weapon toward the floor.

"No, no, no! You gotta hold it like a man, boy!" Dad said.

He reached around Lane and grabbed both of his wrists. He forced Lane's left hand onto the gun so he held it firmly. He lifted his arms so the barrel pointed away from Lane's chest and aimed directly at the mirrored doors of the closet across from them. Lane looked at the reflection and saw his father's woozy expression as he squeezed his right eye shut and placed Lane's index finger on the trigger. He pulled the hammer back with his thumb and raised Lane's arms a few inches higher.

"Now, you gotta squeeze the trigger, kiddo. Don't pull it. Squuuuueeeeeeeeeeze it," he said softly.

Lane started to shiver and his hands were slimy and wet.

"My hands are starting to sweat," Lane said.

"I don't care about your fucking hands."

"But Dad—"

"Shhhhh. Don't say anything, Lane. Just squuuuuueeeeeeeeze..."

"I don't want to, I'm sca—"

"SQUEEZE THE GODDAMN TRIGGER OR I'LL BEAT YOUR FUCKING FACE!"

Lane looked from his father's glassy-eye to the stuffed boy's plastic eye as it laid across the room, and he squeezed the trigger.

2.

Lane stared into his fractured reflection in the shattered closet door as he heard his mother scream from the other room, "My sickness! My sickness!"

"Oh no," Lane whispered.

"My god! Help me! Help me!" Mom screeched manically.

Lane looked to Dad. He was totally unaware of anything that had occurred. "It was loaded?" Lane asked.

There was no response from Dad. Lane leapt from his lap, dropped the gun on the floor, and ran to the kitchen. Mom was flailing around knocking pots and plates onto the floor. She was clutching her head with her hands and Lane noticed a bit of blood dripping through her fingers.

"Oh, Lane!" Mom shouted as she saw him enter, "Thank God you're here! Your father tried to murder me!"

She pulled her hand away from her head and pointed at a small, bleeding wound above her right ear, "He shot me!"

"Oh, Mom... I don't..." Lane said.

"It was an accident!" Dad said as he walked into the room. He squinted his empty eyes to look at Mom's wound, "You're fine!"

Mom frantically turned to Lane, "The sickness, Lane! The sickness! He pierced the skin. The air... it's leaking into the air... my god, Lane! Cover your mouth. I don't know what this power will do to you!" She covered Lane's mouth and nose with her hand and frantically scanned the kitchen. She spotted a plastic bag on the floor, grabbed it, and pulled it over Lane's head, "So it can't enter your lungs! Malicious! Air-borne! It could take over the whole neighborhood!"

"But Mom..." Lane said while trying to pull the bag away from his face.
"No, Lane!" she shouted. "You could die! You can't breathe this air! Sickness! It's everywhere!"
"Mom, you don't under—" Lane began.
"We have to get to the hospital!" she screamed. "You have to drive me!"
"But Mom, I can't—"
"Come on!" She grabbed his wrist and yanked him toward the door, "Before it's too late!"

As they were on their way out of the door Lane's father shouted, "Good riddance! Hope they amputate your whole fucking head for ruining my life!"
"I'm calling the cops as soon as I get back!" Lane's mother replied.
"See if I care!" his father said. "I am the cops! They should arrest you for being a manipulative bitch!"

Lane's mother slammed the door and dragged Lane to the car. "You have to drive, Lane!" she said, "I can't! I can't do it in this state of mind! I could die!"
"Mom, I can't drive!" he said through the plastic, "I don't know how."
"It's easy! You can do it. I know you can! I can't do it! You have to! You have to do it!"
"But Mom..." he said as she chucked him into the driver's seat.
She jumped in the passenger's side and handed him the keys,

"Put those here," she said, pointing to the ignition, "put it in R here," pointing to the shifter, "press the gas, the long skinny one down there, then, when we're out of the driveway, put it in D, hit the gas, and we're off. Easy, right?"

The plastic bag was fogging up, "I don't think I can—"

"Please, Lane. I could die."

Lane stared at his mother and took a deep breath, sucking the plastic into his mouth. He exhaled it out and turned to the windshield, "Okay."

"Thank you, Lane. You just saved my life."

Lane placed the key in the ignition and started the engine. He slowly slid the shifter into reverse and gently pressed the gas pedal. The monster of a car crept backward like a boulder rolling down the side of a mountain. As he reached the street, Lane went for the brake pedal but accidentally hit the gas again. The car seemed to leap into the air and slammed into a car parked across the street.

"Oh no!" Lane screamed.

His mother turned back and checked the other car, the door was crushed like a soda can.

"Here we go!" she shouted, threw the car into drive, and pressed Lane's foot onto the pedal with her own. The car launched onto the road, the engine screaming like an old man on a roller coaster.

Lane's hands melted into the wheel as he tried to keep the roaring beast on the road.

"Faster! Go faster!" his mother screamed and pressed the pedal against the cigarette butt covered floor. Lane squinted through the plastic as the car tore through an intersection, nearly missing a collision with a dump truck and a school bus.

"These assholes are gonna kill us!" she yelled. She turned to Lane, "No one understands the dangers, Lane! No one! Not your father, not the cops, no one! We are alone in this world! We are doomed to be alone forever! Don't ever forget that! Nothing will ever be okay, Lane! Not as long as we're us! Do you understand that?" She tugged Lane's arm, "Do you understand me?"

Lane slowly, listlessly turned his head to his mother and whispered, "I can't breathe..." his eyes fluttered and rolled backward as his hands slunk from the wheel and his body slid into unconsciousness.

"Lane!" his mother grabbed his head. She looked into the plastic and yelled again, "Lane! Wake up, kiddo! Wake up, Lane!" She was so concerned that she barely noticed that the car had driven off the road, crashed through a fence, and had become airborne. Once the car smashed into a tree, flipped over, and bashed into the ground, she got the idea.

Lane's mother pulled him from the wreckage. She breathlessly looked around, pausing to stare at the spinning tire of the overturned car. She touched her nose and felt the warm, grainy mix of blood and dirt dripping from her busted lip. She looked at Lane as he lay on the ground, his head in a plastic bag and his thrift shop suit covered in filth. She pulled the bag from his head and pressed her ear to his nose. Nothing. She moved to his chest. Nothing. Tears filled her eyes as she slowly raised her head and placed her hands on the sides of her son's face.
"I'm sorry, Lane," she whispered. She then took a deep, unsteady breath, and ran away.

And Lane was alone. Lane was always alone.

3.

Nothing but the leaves and the sky. That's all he saw.

Lane was confused. He was scared. He couldn't remember what happened. He felt the earth under his back and the throbbing in his head. He pressed a palm against his eyebrow and slowly sat up, his joints creaking like the wooden floor of an old house. He saw the car resting on its crushed roof. The front tire rotated, whirling on and on, and Lane stared, momentarily hypnotized. He brought his hand to his nose and felt the blood that had run down to his chin. He looked to his chest and saw that his tie was severed and stained with drips from his nose. He looked to the car again and saw the other half of the tie, hanging in tatters from the broken passenger's side window. On the ground, next to Lane's other hand was the plastic bag, stained with blood and dirt. He lifted it to his face and looked through it, like he was examining an expensive jewel. He remembered. He remembered the bag. He remembered his mom. He remembered the shooting and the sickness and his dad and the pistol.   He   remembered   the   crash.

Fear raced through his body as he thought of his mother. Where had she gone? Was she okay? Did she go home?

But he quickly came to another thought, why did she leave me? She's my mother and she left me. Why would she do that?

His eyes welled and he held his breath. "She's my mother... and she left me," he said softly exhaling. And he pressed his hands against his face, and cried.

4.

Lane stepped through the doorway and felt the tension in the house. It was like he was walking underwater. His breathing slowed and he couldn't move freely. There was a smell he couldn't place, a smell that spoke to a part of his brain that had never been spoken to before. The only word that spun through his mind to describe this smell was "bad." Something bad had happened in this house. Something bad had happened and Lane could sense it. He felt it like a rain of needles on his face. Bad things grew, were eaten, chewed up, and spit out in this house. Lane knew it, and he was afraid.

The couches were flipped. Clothes were everywhere. Pots and pans and plates and bowls were broken and scattered all over the kitchen. The dining room table was bashed into splinters and holes decorated the walls like a dalmatian's coat. Chaos and terror was littered around him. He felt like five thousand pounds were resting upon his head. He wanted to run. He wanted to run as far away as possible. He wanted to cry again. He wanted to scream. He wanted to scream and cry and run. But first, he wanted to know. He wanted to know what had happened. And in order to know, he had to be brave. He had to hold back the fear and hold back the screams and hold back the cries, and take a big-time breath and suck it all down and muster up enough to say two words. And he did. And he spoke.

"Mom? Dad?"

No answer. Only the tension. Only the remnants of chaos.

"Mom? Are you here?" he said again. "Dad?"
He walked through the living room toward the bedrooms, carefully stepping over the broken house things. "Mom?" he called again, "Dad? Is anyone here?"

He looked in the bathroom. The tub was running. It had overfilled and was spilling on the floor. The sink was cracked in half and was spouting water like a fire hydrant on an inner-city block during a hot summer day. The medicine chest was ripped from the wall. Bottles of prescription pills were thrown about. Cough medicine stained the floor in a pool that made Lane think horrible thoughts about what he might possibly find somewhere in the house.

He looked in Mom and Dad's room. The bed was upside down and the mattress shredded. Cotton and feathers from pillows covered the floor. It looked like the North Pole set at the mall during Christmas-time, except in this world the elves were fed up and decided to riot.

He knew there was only one room left. He didn't want to look but he had to. He opened the door to the Cube of Doom. It was as he left it. Still depressing. Still humid. Still rotten with silverfish. And though it wasn't destroyed, there was an addition: a video camera set up on a tripod that aimed at an empty chair. It was attached by wires to Lane's tiny television. The fuzzy image on the screen showed the chair. Next to the chair was an empty prescription pill bottle and an empty bottle of something called Lonely Sparrow Whiskey. Lane examined the camera and discovered that it was still on and recording. He pressed stop and rewound the tape. When it reached the beginning he pressed play and watched the TV screen. He saw his father walk from the camera and sit in the chair. He was holding his handgun Psycho. His pupils were the size of nickels and he was red-faced and sweaty.

"I'm sorry, kiddo," he said from the television. He spoke directly to the camera, directly to Lane. His voice was slightly higher than normal and his words slurred. He seemed like he was holding back vomit. Like it was climbing from his stomach to his mouth and he was trying to keep it down but it wanted to fight through the words. He said, "I'm sorry for all the things I do. I'm sorry for the mistakes I've made. I'm sorry for the mistakes I haven't yet made. I'm sorry for the mistakes that I'm going to make, and I'm sorry for the mistakes that you're going to make. This is my fault. This will always be my fault and I'm sorry for that. I'm sorry for me. And for you. And for this. I'm sorry, son. I'm sorry for everything."

Lane sat on the floor and frowned as he watched and processed and felt the sick swirl in his stomach.

"I never wanted this life. I wanted to travel. I wanted to see things. I wanted to live somewhere else. Somewhere different. Somewhere like the Netherlands or something." He looked toward the floor and chuckled. "They say the Dutch are a happy people," he said. "But I didn't get to do that. I didn't get to do anything. And that's no good. So here's what I'm gonna do. I'm gonna go somewhere and get some dinner and have a meal and have a smoke and have a beer. And I'm gonna come home. I'm gonna come home and I'm gonna watch TV. I'm gonna watch TV like you're watching TV right now, and I'm gonna have a laugh at that sitcom with that dumb kid. And I'm gonna drink whiskey and have a smoke again." He looked toward the floor, frowned, took a breath, and raised his head. "Then I'm gonna lay in bed and I'm gonna kill myself. That's something that I need to do, because you don't know what I'm like, kiddo." His eyes closed like a pair of roll-top desks and he started laughing. The muscles in Lane's face twitched as if the corners of his mouth were pulled from below.

Dad continued with a grin, "Soon as I come back, good ol' Psycho here and me are gonna have a time."

He looked down and sighed.

"Just wanted to say goodbye, kiddo. You're a good boy. I'll miss you."

He stared into the camera as his eyes glazed with tears. "I'm sorry, Lane. I mean it, too. It's not gonna be easy for you. It never will be."

And he stood and walked away from the camera. He dropped Psycho next to the doorway and left the room. Lane turned away from the TV and saw the gun. He looked back to the screen and saw only the chair. He pressed stop on the camera, ejected the tape, walked to the door, took the gun, and left the room.

He found a shovel in the shed, dug a hole as deep as he could, and dropped the gun and video tape in. As he covered them over he thought of his mother. He wondered if he would ever see her again. He wondered if she was alive. He hoped she was and he hoped his father would come home and be too lazy to end his life after he couldn't find his gun. He hoped he would sleep it off and wake up and watch TV and be done with it. He hoped these things were true.

And he patted the dirt flat and returned the shovel to the shed.

CHAPTER TWENTY-NINE

The Psycho Killer Down the Street Part 9: Oh No!

Daniel Groff Jr.
Grade 3
January 31, 1990

"Oh my god it's you! The Psycho Killer Down the Street!"

"I'm back and I'm mad!" he said and pulled out his Psycho knife. "You killed me four times. I didn't like that. Get ready to taste death, you little S.O.B." He threw his knife at me. It got me in the leg. He punched me in the face and he kicked the knife deeper in.

"Ahhhh!" I screamed.

"You've been hurtin' my friend Satan. Don't do that anymore!" he said. He punched me in the face seven times then kicked me again. He slammed my head against a wall five times. He threw me against the ground and kicked me in the stomach and in the face. I was bleeding from everywhere. He slammed my head against the ground. He pulled the knife out of my leg and slashed my face, shoulder, arm, and other leg. He smacked me in the face and punched me in the stomach. He grabbed my throat and started choking me. I grabbed his knife and stabbed him in the stomach. I smacked the knife deeper and deeper and deeper in. I punched him in the face. He let go. He grabbed me and threw me over a fire pit. He pushed my head down. The flames started blowing up. I kicked him in the leg and flipped him over my head. He fell into the fire. "Ahhhhh!" he screamed. He burned away.

Then Satan came walking toward me. His horns were all cracked. He roared like a lion. He picked up Psycho Killer's knife and threw it at me.

"ARGH!" It hit me in the stomach and I got woozy. I think it's over. There goes my second chance. I failed.

The end?

CHAPTER THIRTY

From Troubled to Me

I think this is happening because I live within myself. I am a character who lives as me inside me. There was a troubled boy, but now there is a detective man that lives as me inside me and he represents me and he's now the real me. He's going to change me. He's going to change the world. He's okay. When I'm not okay, he's okay. And if he's okay, I'm okay. We're okay. And the world is going to get better. I know it is. Anger is done. Cynicism is gone. Things are going to change. Things are going to get good soon. The world will be right soon. I will be right soon. That's why there's this man inside me. He represents something. He represents a positive way of life. He represents everything that's me. There's part of me that feels good. And that part of me can come out and become all of me. There's part of me that's okay. There's a detective man inside me named Lane Laszlo and he is going to solve a mystery forever because that is the brave thing to do.

That is what we need him to do.

That is what I need him to do.

So I type.

CHAPTER THIRTY-ONE

Elvis Cries Coffee

After reading, Lane Laszlo lowered the pages and frowned. He felt lost. He felt uncomfortable. He felt sad. He felt wrong. To right his head, he lit some Nag Champa incense and sat cross-legged in his recliner. He sipped coffee from his favorite mug. The one with Elvis on it. It was a souvenir from Graceland. Lane always wanted to go to Graceland, but he never did. He got that mug from a thrift shop for a dollar and figured that was as close as he'd ever get. So now he watched TV and thought about Abby and her nose and her face and her screaming. He thought about the story and that life and wondered about the real. Lane Laszlo thought of his work and thought of her and thought of the change and didn't move. He stared at the screen and watched some sitcom about some kid with a stupid hat and a girl who didn't know he was alive.

An audience laughed.

The people clapped.

And the show went on.

"I fucking hate sitcoms," Lane said.

He knew new things.

New things were changing the old things.

He knew these new things in a new way.

It was strange for him.

He took a sip and stared. He stared at the King's mug on the mug of the King and saw the coffee slide in a tiny stream down the ceramic side over his face and saw a tear drip from The King's eye. "Elvis cries coffee," he said with a smirk, "good title for something."

He set the mug on the folding table next to the chair and picked up the pages. Those pages. Those pages that were about Lane Laszlo and the things that happened.

He decided to take shower and used patchouli soap, the natural kind from the expensive store that smelled like that He-Man figure that looked like a skunk. He smelled like the hippies that passed him on the street. He smelled like someone else. He wasn't sure who was supposed to be. He knew who he was and he wasn't him anymore.

But he waited.

He thumbed the pages and looked at the words and waited.

Lane Laszlo let It down. Lane Laszlo let himself down. He was not Lane Laszlo and he knew this. He knew who he was supposed to be. He knew the Everything made the choice. It pushed the one that It needed. He knew there was something inside him. Lane knew this world needed whatever it was.

He didn't know how he knew these things. But he knew these things.

Imprints. They felt like imprints. Like a stamp from somewhere slammed these things into him. Like a bureaucratic nightmare. Stamping, "approved." Stamping, "rejected." Stamping, "life." Stamping, "existence."

He was hungry. He wanted a hamburger. He hadn't eaten

meat in what felt like a long time and he wanted blood. He was losing weight and he was feeling tired and he wanted animal. He was depleted and deficient and unhappy and confused.

But he held.

He waited.

He stared.

His breath shallow. His heart fluttering. His hands shaking. The sweat pooled in the seat of his pants and his toes formed fists. His stomach churned and fired with random bursts of pain. He hoped it was gas. He hoped it would go away. It wasn't gas. It was a need. It was a desire. He wanted to make it right. He wanted to solve the case.

He was supposed to make a difference. He was supposed to be the one. He was supposed to change it all. He was special. He was real. He was the good thing.

And he closed his eyes and touched the burn on his face. "I have to see Abby again," he said. But he didn't know why.

CHAPTER THIRTY-TWO

The Psycho Killer Down the Street Part 10: It Might Be Over

Daniel Groff Jr.
Grade 3
February 14, 1990

"No! No! No! It's not over." I screamed and jumped to my feet. I pulled the knife out of my stomach. I threw it and it hit Satan in the head. He just growled and pulled it out. He took the knife and charged me with it. I moved out of the way and kicked him in the stomach and punched him in the back. He punched me in the face. I was knocked out instantly because the Psycho Killer beat me so bad.

Hours and hours passed. I opened my eyes. "Where am I?" I said.

Satan walked in. I was strapped to a table. He untied me and threw me out the door. He grabbed my throat and said, "You killed my good friend Psycho Kill—"

"Hey, I ain't dead!" Psycho Killer said. "It'll take a lot more than that to kill me."

Satan said, "Get 'em, Psycho!"

He grabbed my throat. I punched him in the face. I kicked him in the head. I stood up and I hit his head against a wall. I headbutted him and he started bleeding. He grabbed my face and pushed me back. Then Satan came to me he stabbed me through my shoulder. Satan smacked me, then Psycho smacked me, then Satan, then Psycho. They each smashed my head against the wall five times. They both swung at me. I ducked and they punched each other. I jumped up and smashed their heads together. Satan disappeared.

It was me and Psycho. Old friends.

Psycho charged. I jumped up and kicked him in the face. I punched him in the stomach. He grabbed me and smashed me against a wall and punched me in the face six times. He kicked me in the stomach. Then he hit my head against the wall. He threw me off a fifteen foot cliff. I broke my wrist and cut my head open. I cracked a big sharp rock and stabbed him in the face. He rolled over. He's dead I hope.

The end?

CHAPTER THIRTY-THREE

Real Happiness

I'm not tragic. I'm not deep. I'm not broken. I'm not negative. Not anymore. Positivity is the thing now. Hope is the stuff now. Cynicism is gone now. Hate is over. Fear is over. It's all over. It's all over except for happiness and real and real happiness. Happiness is here because happiness is the way to happiness. And we need happiness for happiness to survive. Happiness is Lane Laszlo. Happiness is reality. Lane Laszlo is real happiness and Lane Laszlo is reality. Real reality. Lane Laszlo is there and I can feel him and I can get him out. I can write him out.

Our higher selves can recognize our higher selves as our lower selves can recognize our lower selves. This is where the connection comes from. We are united somewhere. Somewhere, we are already friends, already lovers, already family. This is what's important. This is what we tap into. This is the Everything. This place, this somewhere. This is what we are looking for. This somewhere, this place is where we will go. We are almost ready. We are almost ready for the journey.

When you meet someone and you feel that completeness, you're tapping in. You have found the place. You have found it, you have felt it. You've experienced the feeling of a cellular structure breaking down into its basic parts and entwining with the cells of another. We are all made of beauty. We are made of happiness. That's why this feeling feels happy, because that's what it is. We are happiness. We are real. We are feeling. It's a glorious time to be alive because we are connected. We have felt the cellular breakdown. We have tapped in. We have experienced neverendingness. We have experienced the Everything. Now, we need to go there forever. That is where we will live. That is where we will be forever and ever and ever and ever. Neverending. Always.

And so I drink.

And so I type.

CHAPTER THIRTY-FOUR

Brittle and Dry

Lane parked in front of 7 Milberg Place and walked across what was now the dry and brittle lawn. The house was different this time. It was old. It was moldy. It was unloved.

He knocked on the front door and was surprised when it creaked open. He poked his head inside and called, "Abby?"

There was no response. Lane stepped through the doorway and walked into the formerly comforting living room to find the furniture flipped, the walls ravaged with holes, and misery in the air.

"Feels familiar," he said. "So familiar that..."

Lane pulled the pages that Abby gave him on his last visit and read aloud while walking through the house and seeing what the words described. "The couches were flipped. Clothes were everywhere. Pots and pans and plates and bowls were broken and scattered all over the kitchen. The dining room table was bashed into splinters and holes decorated the walls like a dalmatian's coat. Chaos and terror was littered around him. He felt like five thousand pounds were resting upon his head. He wanted to run. He wanted to run as far away as possible. He wanted to cry again. He wanted to scream. He wanted to scream and cry and run. But first, he wanted to know. He wanted to know what had happened. And in order to know, he had to be brave. He had to hold back the fear and hold back the screams and hold back the cries, and take a big-time breath and suck it all down and muster up enough to say two words. And he did. And he spoke."

"Hello? Abby?" Lane called.

Nothing.

He returned to the page, "No answer. Only the tension. Only the remnants of chaos," he read. "He walked through the living room toward the bedrooms, carefully stepping over the broken house things," he said. "Abby?" he called again, "Is anyone here?"

He continued to read.

"He looked in the bathroom. The tub was running. It had overfilled and was spilling on the floor. The sink was cracked in half and was spouting water like a fire hydrant on an inner-city block during a hot summer day. The medicine chest was ripped from the wall. Bottles of prescription pills were thrown about. Cough medicine stained the floor in a pool that made Lane think horrible thoughts about what he might possibly find somewhere in the house."

He read on, "He looked in Mom and Dad's room. The bed was upside down and the mattress shredded. Cotton and feathers from pillows covered the floor. It looked like the North Pole set at the mall during Christmas-time, except in this world the elves were fed up and decided to riot."

And on, "He knew there was only one room left. He didn't want to look, but he had to. He opened the door to the Cube of Doom."

But Lane was unable to open this door. It was blocked. Blocked by something. He pressed his shoulder against it and pushed, but he couldn't open it.

Lane consulted the pages and saw that the story moved

beyond his reality. "Well, that's a fucking bummer," he said and turned to a different door and opened it. It revealed a set of wooden stairs that led to a basement. "Maybe this is something," Lane said and walked through.

At least in this reality, he was calling the shots, Lane thought. There was no book dictating his moves. It was Lane and Lane alone.

So he continued his descent.

Lane Laszlo stepped down onto the wood slowly and carefully. Each step creaked like a squawking parrot. Each step begged him for a cracker. Each step told him to fuck himself in an adorable little cartoon voice. Each step led him to somewhere and to something that made his heart pump a little faster. It was dark, it was uncertain, it was confusing.

As his foot hit the cement floor, he realized that he was in the dark. That kind of dark that's afraid of itself again. He reached into his messenger bag and pulled the policeman badge Zippo and flicked the flame. A halo surrounded him and illuminated the nastiness. It was a basement that looked like a basement. An ugly basement. There were things, there was moisture, there was darkness, there was creepiness, there was crap.

He held the flame like a torch in a jungle. He scanned the walls but found nothing but exposed beams and fiberglass. There was dampness in the air and he felt it on his skin and in his hair. He walked the perimeter of the room, ducking ducts and stepping over moldy cardboard boxes that drooped from the wetness of the underneath world. He thought of rats and mice and roaches and silverfish. He thought of snakes, bats, goblins, and darkness. He thought of scary things and creatures and monsters and slime. He started to scare himself. He started to shake. He started to breathe. He thought about leaving and turned to go when he found a doorway tucked in the back corner of the basement that led to another, smaller room.

The lighter lit the way as he stepped through the door. He

noticed the walls were decorated with pieces of paper and scraps and junk. He held out the flame and approached a sign written in magic marker that hung in the center of the wall. It said:

ELECTRICITY IS THE PROBLEM AND THE SOLUTION!!!

He slid his fingers under the sign and pulled it from the wall. He read it again and looked up and see that beneath it was a fuse box. He dropped the sign, opened the small door, and flipped every switch.

POP!

The lights burst to life and they were much brighter than he thought they would be. Fluorescent bulbs were installed in the ceiling which gave the basement the sterile and nauseating feeling of a mental institution. The dirt and grime and ugliness on the floor came into view. He looked around and noticed that the walls were covered with makeshift wallpaper made from photos, newspaper clippings, sloppily handwritten notes, and other cliché, crazy people things like:

THIS IS THE ONE.

DON'T BELIEVE IN ANYONE OR ANYTHING.

IT WAS HIM BUT IT WAS ALSO ME AND IT WAS ALSO YOU.

WHAT ELSE DO I NEED?

Empty pill bottles were scattered about a throw rug on the floor like spent shells from a machine gun. He bent over to pick one up and felt an incredible warmth from beneath the rug, like an oven. Like an oven under the floor, under the house.

He stood and read the bottle.

REALITALL

TAKE 2 TABLETS WHENEVER MALADJUSTMENT OCCURS.
MAY CAUSE SEVERE DISINTEGRATION OF THE MIND. TAKE WITH FOOD.

"Maladjustment?" he said with pause then slipped the bottle into his pocket.

There was a workbench that was covered with various tools, cigarette butts, pens, paper, empty bottles, manila folders, candy bar wrappers, a bowl stained blackish, and an old typewriter. A stuffed doll of a sad looking boy with one plastic eye and its stomach torn to shreds sat atop of a book called *Learning to Speak Dutch for Fucking Morons*. A stack of typed pages rested next to the typewriter and one, half-typed page remained in the machine.

It said:

Kiddo,

The pages here represent all I have done. I know I was not good. I know I was not there. But it was for this. Now this is for you.

Daniel Groff is a person who was sent to me. He was sent from It up above through the thing down below and put in me to help me investigate Everything. He helped me find my way. He helped me find my me and my peace and my happiness.

I'm a detective, boy. Like you. I've been investigating a case for a long time and I need help now. I need you.

Daniel Groff is a "fictional" character created by It and forced into my soul through the thing down below to show me the path of Everything. He was conjured by It and delivered to me through the place in the basement. I was battling depression and fighting off the effects of a time-shifting and reality-bending existence and Daniel Groff helped me my find my path. He's a writer and a man and he makes sense to me. He makes sense of me. He was sent as a fully formed and fully realized human and he's always ready to tackle my problems and lead the way. He can help you too, kiddo. He's here for us. For us Laszlos. He's our guy. He's our good guy. Our good thing.

Let him in, kiddo.

Let him be with you, kiddo.

Let him be you, kiddo.

It's not always going to make sense, but that's okay. It's not supposed to make sense and even if it does, it doesn't. Making sense is making fiction out of fact. Remember that. Forget sense. Forget fiction. Forget fact. Remember Daniel Groff.

Find him.

Feel him.

Love him.

I am him.

You are him.

Be him.

Best,
Dad

Who is this Dad and why is he speaking to me like this? Lane thought. It's like he knew him or something.

"Whatever," Lane said and turned to the throw rug in the center of the floor. For some reason, the warmth that was emanating from beneath it seemed worthy of further examination. "Hell, maybe you are an investigator after all, Laszlo?" Lane chuckled.

He yanked the rug away revealing a trap door with a metal

handle.

"Well, I'll be god damned," he said and grabbed the handle, pulled open the door, and descended the stairs.

CHAPTER THIRTY-FIVE

The Star

I would like hope and wellness and happiness to be my profession. I think that's where Lane Laszlo comes from. That's why he was given to me. He somehow showed up in me and is telling me his story and now I have this need to get him into the world. I don't know where he came from but he's part of me. I don't know if he was always there. I suppose he was. Maybe I missed him. Maybe I ignored him. Maybe I disregarded him. It feels like he arrived though. It feels like he was delivered that day. I don't know where characters come from. I don't know how they get there. It feels like they're there already, but I don't think that's possible. I would have noticed Lane before. I would have been aware of him. I would have gotten him out sooner. But Lane showed and Lane made me feel different and I want to tell his story to people. I want to write a book featuring Lane and his cases. I want to write a mystery. I think Lane could star in a whole series of books. I think Lane could star in a TV show. I would probably make a fortune off Lane. But that's not the most important part of the whole thing. The whole thing is the hope and the change and the happiness and the wellness. The whole thing is the reality. The whole thing is the completeness. I could get Lane out. Lane could be free. I would be free if Lane was free. And you would be free if I was free.

Are you listening to me, kiddo. Are you here with me?
We should free Lane together.
Do you hear me?

Are you me?

CHAPTER THIRTY-SIX

The Pyshco Killer Down the Street Part 11: I Must Destroy Him

Daniel Groff Jr.
Grade 3
February 28, 1990

Suddenly Satan reappeared.

He said, "Men, attack!" The black demons jumped on me. One slashed my face and another bit me. I jumped up and spun kicked all the demons. They disappeared. I jumped at Satan. He caught me and whipped me against the wall. He punched me in the back then hit my head against the wall. He grabbed my throat and he picked me up. Satan let go and dropped me. He kicked me in the stomach and then in the head. He grabbed my left hand. He started twisting it and pulled until he tore my hand off!

"AHHHHHHHHHHHHHHHH!!!! You ugly MOTHER!" I screamed.

I got up and ran through a door to find myself at a river. It didn't look like the kind of river you would see in Hell. But that doesn't mean it wasn't. Especially since I saw an old "friend" standing by the water. It was him. The Psycho Killer Down the Street. It was now time to finish this.

To be concluded.

CHAPTER THIRTY-SEVEN

The River

Lane stood at the bank of the river that ran beneath 7 Milberg Place. He noticed bushes neatly planted that grew the same kind of leafy greens and berries that he saw Abby gardening. "This is weird," Lane said as he marched toward one, pulling the Psycho knife from his messenger bag so he could cut some leaves and berries away and investigate closer. When he heard the voice of a child say,

"It's you."

He turned to see a badly battered kid who was around 9 years-old. His nose was bloodied, his face was slashed, his eye was swollen, and at the end of his left wrist was a bloody stump as if his hand had been torn off.

"This ends now, Psycho Killer," the kid yelled and charged toward Lane.

"Wait, wait, wait!" Lane screamed as the kid collided with him and drove him to the ground like a linebacker.

The kid punched Lane in the face five times then kicked him in the stomach. He grabbed his head and beat it against the ground. Lane pushed the kid away and the kid punched him in the face two times and bit his shoulder and made him bleed. Lane was hurt bad.

Lane stood up and said, "You little jerk! Stop attacking me!"

The kid said, "No way, you scarred lunatic! I need to finally beat you!" The kid jumped at Lane and kneed him in the jaw and elbowed him in the face and poked him in the eyes and punched him over and over and over again until Lane fell into the river and was taken away.

He was gone forever.

The end?

CHAPTER THIRTY-EIGHT

Anger

I don't want to feel angry. Anger is a disease. Anger is a disease that needs to be cured and the world needs to be free. Truth is real. Knowledge is real. Reality is the cure. We each have the cure in us and Lane is my cure. I want to be cured. I want to feel fine. I want to feel okay. I want to feel happy. I don't want to write about anger. I don't want to write about fear. I don't want to write about paranoia. I don't want to write about misery. I don't want to write about me. I want to write about him. He's the stuff. He's the good stuff. He's the real stuff. He's the cure. He needs to be free. He needs to be me and I need to be him.

It's almost time for Lane Laszlo.

It's almost time to embrace the Everything.

And so I need to take the next step in finding the good.

And so I type.

And so I drink.

And so I am.

CHAPTER THIRTY-NINE
A Circular Quest

I'm on a path to nowhere now and Lane could lead me to the place of goods things. Honesty. Truth. Intelligence. When added together all those things equal happiness. They equal peace. They equal reality. They equal real reality. Not the reality that appears to us outside the window. That is not reality. That is not real. That is fear. That is ugly. That is stupid. Lane's world is the world that I want. I want honesty. I want wellness.

I read the news. I read about the President and the terrorists and the guns. It makes me sad and scared and angry and annoyed and depressed when I read these things. This world has come apart. This world is full of weirdness. This is world is full of craziness. It's full of spying and shootings and torture and violence. I watch videos of protests and anger and ignorance and teargas grenades. I watch these things and get scared and get sick and think of the change that could come. That's a positive way of thinking. That's a positive thought that I have. My thoughts are nuggets of hope buried in piles of shit. I think of the hope that Lane could bring. I think of how I want the misery to go away. I think of how I want the scary things in this world to melt into liquid and pour into drains and be gone forever.

I think of how I want this world to be right.

I think of how it's time for me to fix it.

I think of how it's time for us to fix it.

It's Lane and I who will do this together by using the words in my face.

It's me who will change.

It's me.

"It's you," I hear a voice say from behind me. I turn to see a soaking wet man with an old suit, a nasty burn on his face, a bloody nose, and the Psycho Killer Down the Street's knife.

"Lane Laszlo?" I say.
"Yeah," he said. "It's me."
"You're here."
"Where is this?"
I shrug.
"Are you the one calling the shots?" Lane said.
I stare at the Psycho blade and notice that Lane Laszlo, my inherited fictional investigator man is trembling. "I don't think anyone is, Lane."
Lane takes a deep breath and frowns. "Well, what am I supposed to investigate then?" he says. "What the fuck am I supposed to figure out?"
I stand and slowly approach Lane. "I think you're supposed to figure out me," I say.
"What's the point of me, then?" he says.
"The point of you is the point of me," I say. "And the point of me is the point of... something. I don't know. But I hope it's good."
Lane looks to the ground. "I don't think that's fair," he says. "I don't think that's right."
"Neither do I," I say. "And I'm not going to pretend that I understand it, because I don't know shit about shit. And I don't think I'll ever know shit about shit. But I do know one thing..."

I grasp his arms and the words spill out of me.

"I know that I'm sorry. I'm sorry for all the things I do. I'm sorry for the mistakes I've made. I'm sorry for the mistakes I haven't yet made. I'm sorry for the mistakes that I'm going to make, and I'm sorry for the mistakes that you're going to make. This is my fault. This will always be my fault and I'm sorry for that. I'm sorry for me. And for you. And for this. I'm sorry, Lane. I'm sorry I broke the Everything."

"Am I even real?" he says.

"I don't know. I don't think there's any way to ever know. I don't think it matters." I smile, "And maybe that's what we have to deal with. That nothing fucking matters. That it's all, all. And that's it."

He looks to the floor and shakes his head. "I don't think that's right," he says.

"But I do," I say. "Because this is all mine. I made this. And I'm sorry about that too."

Lane raises his head and stares into my eyes. "I'm the one who's sorry," he says and he plunges the blade into my head.

A shock of light steals my vision as I stumble backward fall through the trap door, down the fifty or sixty stairs, landing on the ground below.

I force myself to my hands and knees and watch the blood spill onto the grass landing between my splayed fingers. I try to stand as I hear Lane Laszlo descend the stairs and feel my shirt tighten as he grabs a handful of my suit jacket. He drags me toward the river and tosses me into the rushing water.

As it takes me, I'm able to watch Lane Laszlo watch me drift away. And I think that despite it all, this is right. This is change. This is real. This is what's happening now.

And I'm carried away. Away to somewhere that I can only hope is better.

CHAPTER FORTY

Why?

Lane held the knife and felt the warm blood drip on his hand. He grimaced and tossed the blade into the river.

He stood and watched Daniel Groff bob and drift along in the drink, staring back toward Lane with a look that read pathetic to the private investigator. He watched with a mix of remorse and pity until Daniel Groff was finally out of sight.

Finally somewhere else.

Lane felt sorry for what he'd done. He didn't know why he had to do it, but he knew he had to do it. And it was done. And he now had the question that he needed to ask. He knew what he needed to investigate.

Why did Daniel Groff have to die?

And it was time for Lane Laszlo to find the answer.

CHAPTER FORTY-ONE

The Psycho Killer Down the Street Part 12: The End?

Daniel Groff Jr.
Grade 3
March 14, 1990

Finally the Psycho Killer is gone forever. Now I gotta kill Satan. Suddenly he appeared. He picked up a sword and stabbed me in the shoulder. Then he stabbed me in the other shoulder. He tried to stab me in the head but I ducked. I kicked him in the stomach five times. I jumped up and kicked him in the face. I picked up a sword. I stabbed him in the chest six times. Then sliced his throat. I stabbed him in the eye. He grabbed me and threw me up in the air. Satan flew up in the air. He grabbed my throat and smashed me into the wall seven times. He put my right foot in his mouth and bit it off. He hit my head against the ground. I punched him in the face. I kicked him in the head with my left foot. I grabbed his horn and started twisting and pulling.

SNAP! I pulled it off!

I punched him in the face three times. I kicked him in the stomach. He grabbed my throat and he started biting my head. I grabbed the bottom of his mouth and started pulling.

SNAP! I broke his jaw.

I put my fist in his mouth and punched through the back of his head. He picked up the sword and stabbed it into my leg two times. I got up and smacked him in the face and pushed him off a cliff.

BOOM! He hit the ground.

He got back up. He was on his feet. I grabbed the sword and stood. I said, "Satan, you must die!" I jumped at him. "UGHHH!" Satan's sword went through my stomach. I dropped the sword. Satan pulled me off. He laid me on the ground. He picked up the sword. He went to stab me, but suddenly a big blue light shot down and blew Satan away. Satan fell and he was dead. All Hell turned into Heaven. Every one of Satan's demons disappeared. I heard a voice, it said, "You did well." I saw a big white mist come over me. My hand and foot grew back and all my wounds were healed. I succeeded. I destroyed Hell. POOF! I was back in my bed. I had headphones on. It must have been a dream.

I turned around and I saw Satan's shadow on my wall and I heard pots and pans and plates and bowls crashing and screaming from the kitchen.

Oh no! It wasn't a dream!

The End.

Forever?

CHAPTER FORTY-TWO

The Everything

Lane climbed the stairs and entered the small basement room and sat at the typewriter. He scanned the workbench, letting his eyes drift over the pages, the books, the Lonely Sparrow Whiskey bottles, the berries, the nonsense. And he halted on the stuffed boy. That gut-shot boy with one plastic eye. That boy with the saddest eye in the world. And he thought about his story while staring into that black dot and sighed. "I think I know what to call you now," he said.

He reached into his messenger bag and removed the tiny wooden duck that he retrieved from poor Roy's stabbed head and rested it next to the boy.

He grabbed a bottle of Lonely Sparrow Whiskey, sloshed the brown liquid back and forth, and unscrewed the cap. He knocked back a sip and winced from the craziness. It was strong and it was brutal and he needed it like that. He swallowed it down and sighed. Relaxed. Calm. Cool. Collected.

He rested his hands on the keys of the typewriter as Abby rested her hand on his shoulder. He glanced up and she smiled.

"Fix the Everything, Lane."

He nodded. He took a breath. He thought of Daniel Groff's face as it floated away.

And he began to type:

I want to be good now. I want to be right now. I want to be happy now. Happiness can play if you let it out into the yard. Mine's grounded. Mine said, "fuck" and I washed its mouth out with soap and it's in its room. I want to let the happiness out but the happiness needs to learn to stop being such a goddamn smart-ass.

There's peace in me. There's real in me. There's life in me. I think of these things and that means these things are there. If they weren't there, then I wouldn't think of them. I wouldn't even know what they are. Misery is worthless and that's the new way to think. That's the right way to think. That's the way I want to live. That's the way I'm going to live.

Starting now.

Eddie Wright was born in New Jersey. He is the creator and writer of the graphic novel *Tyranny of the Muse* and author of *Broken Bulbs*.

For more visit eddie-wright.com